THIRST

A NOVEL

DEBORAH BLADON

FIRST ORIGINAL EDITION, FEBRUARY 2019

Copyright © 2019 by Deborah Bladon

ISBN-13: 9781796856149
eBook ISBN: 9781926440545

Book & cover design by Wolf & Eagle Media

www.deborahbladon.com

Also by Deborah Bladon

THE OBSESSED SERIES
THE EXPOSED SERIES
THE PULSE SERIES
THE VAIN SERIES
THE RUIN SERIES
IMPULSE
SOLO
THE GONE SERIES
FUSE
THE TRACE SERIES
CHANCE
THE EMBER SERIES
THE RISE SERIES
HAZE
SHIVER
TORN
THE HEAT SERIES
MELT
THE TENSE DUET
SWEAT
TROUBLEMAKER
WORTH
HUSH
BARE
WISH
SIN
LACE

Chapter 1

Dexie

"I don't understand why you haven't invested in window coverings for this place."

I turn to see my friend, Sophia Wolf, standing next to one of the large windows in my new apartment.

"I like the light," I answer quickly. "Besides, in my rental agreement it says that the building's superintendent will supply blinds and install them. The man is busy. I don't want to bother him about it."

"You pay rent which means it's his job to keep you happy."

Spoken from the lips of a woman who lives in a luxurious apartment with her novelist husband and daughter.

"Don't worry about it, Sophia." I put a cardboard box on the kitchen counter. "I really like this place. It's cheaper than my last apartment and there's a lot more room."

"I can't argue with that." She takes in the sprawling space. "Are you thinking of setting up your workstation over there?"

I haven't given it any serious thought yet because my time is limited. I work full-time in the marketing department for a cosmetics company and part-time helping Sophia with her clothing line.

My purse design business has yet to take off, but I'm determined to change that. I've put out some feelers to try and find a private investor for my company.

Supplies aren't cheap and even though I have a steady stream of customers willing to pay for my one-of-a-kind handmade purses, there's not enough cash coming in to take my business to the next level.

"I'm going to get all my stuff unpacked and then I'll figure that out."

She taps her heel on the hardwood floor. "That makes sense."

I point at a lamp on a table near where she's standing. "Can you turn that on? It's getting dark."

She hits the switch on the lamp and it instantly fills the room with soft light. "I have one more concern and then I swear I'll shut up."

I don't look at her as I open a box filled with dishes. "What?"

"Your bed is right in front of that window. Aren't you worried that your neighbors will watch you while you sleep?"

I picked this apartment because it has a loft feel to it. My bed is visible from my kitchen and the main living space. The only area that is separated by walls and a door is the bathroom.

I'm not shy. I've slept here for the past four nights and I haven't bothered to look out any of the windows to see if the people in the building next to mine are looking in.

"This is Manhattan." I stop what I'm doing and scan the exterior wall and the arched windows that face the building next door. "People are too busy to stare in here."

"What if you bring a guy home, Dex?"

"A guy?" I pause as I tuck a lock of my pink-streaked blonde hair behind my ear. "You're worried that my neighbors are going to watch me having sex? Is that what you're asking?"

She laughs. "It's a possibility, no?"

"Not right now." I give an exaggerated shrug. "I don't have time to meet men. You can rest easy tonight knowing that my neighbors won't be getting a free show."

Her dark brown hair sways as she crosses the room to pick up her purse from where she tossed it onto the corner of my bed when she got here. It's one of my latest designs. Sophia is my walking talking billboard and so far, I've had a few customers seek me out because of her.

"I have to get home." She shoulders the navy blue bag. It's a perfect complement to the red blouse and white pants she's wearing. "I need to make dinner. Do you want to come by for a bite?"

I look around the apartment. I have too much to do tonight. There's no way I can spare the time it would take to get to her place, eat, visit and then trudge back here. "Thanks, but I'll pass."

"I'll talk to you later in the week." She hugs me tightly. "Call me if you spot any peeping Toms."

"Will do." My reply is swift. "I'm not sure what you'll do about it, but I'll shoot you a text if I catch one."

***

I arch my back in a stretch as I finally put away the last of my dishes. I don't own a lot, but my mismatched collection of plates, bowls and glasses is enough for me. I've never thrown an elaborate dinner party. I only cook the basics. All of my spare time is devoted to my passion. If I'm not working on one of my handbags, I'm thinking about elements for the next design.

I ate a bowl of cereal for dinner after Sophia left, taking a spoonful in between unpacking boxes.

I've accomplished more tonight than I thought I would. I glance at my phone sitting on the worn laminate countertop and realize that it's nearing midnight.

Since I need to be at my office at Matiz Cosmetics nine hours from now, sleep has to be next on my schedule.

I hurry toward the bed. It's not the most comfortable I've ever slept in, but it's large and right now it's calling my name.

Just as I'm about to tug my pink T-shirt over my head and unbutton my jeans, I turn to the windows.

The building next door is close. It's also home to many apartments with dozens of windows.

Several of the windows are shuttered with curtains and blinds. Subtle hints of light peek around the edges. A few apartments don't have any window coverings and they're backlit enough that I can make out what's happening in the homes of my neighbors.

Television sets flicker, a woman dances past a window, and then my gaze settles on the apartment directly across from mine.

I know that the low light coming from the lamp in the corner makes me visible to the person standing with their back to me.

There's a light on in their apartment too. It's not too bright, more of a gentle glow that casts just enough warmth that I can see the shape of a man. He's tall with broad shoulders.

When he turns, I lean closer to the window to get a better look.

He does the same. His gaze locks with mine and a shiver of excitement runs through me.

He's gorgeous. He has dark hair and a chiseled jaw.

He slides his suit jacket off, and I long for him to open each of the buttons on his white dress shirt.

He does. He unbuttons them one-by-one and as he reaches the last, he stops and rests both hands on the glass.

I hold my breath wanting more, but then he turns abruptly, walks away from the window and leaves me wondering when I'll see him again.

Chapter 2

Rocco

"The ask is substantial, Silas." I glance at the man sitting next to me. "What makes you think I'm interested in something like this?"

He moves to get a look at what's displayed on my laptop screen. "We both made a fortune on Jewel Jinx. History is about to repeat itself."

Jewel Jinx was a once-in-a-lifetime investment. I put a mid-six figures check in his hand and a year later, I was depositing one in my account for ten times that. My equity in the company has paid off in spades. I'm still receiving bi-monthly payments because the gaming app has a strong base of diehard fans that haven't deleted it to leap on the next craze.

"This is nothing like Jewel Jinx." I lift a hand and point at the laptop screen and the graphic that was included in the presentation package he sent to me via email late last night.

"That's the beauty of it, Rocco." He blows a strand of blond hair out of his eyes. "We're jumping into a solid space with a new twist on what people are craving. I'm telling you this is going to be bigger than Jewel Jinx."

I trust his intuition, but I trust my consultant, Lilly Parker's, insight more.

She's a tech wizard and when I ran the idea for Jewel Jinx past her two years ago, she was so excited about the app that she bought in too. Her percentage was a lot less than mine, but she's made more than pocket change on the deal.

"How married are you to the name of this thing?" I rake a hand through my dark brown hair.

"Word Wize?" he hisses the *z* out for emphasis. "There are millions of game apps. We need to stand out. The name does that."

It rubs me the wrong way. I've invested in dozens of ventures since I retired from professional gambling. I've always listened to the pitch, considered the pros and cons and relied on my gut instinct to guide me.

If I don't feel a connection to the product, business or person pitching their idea to me, I'll bow out.

I'm not prepared to do that yet. Silas didn't steer me wrong with Jewel Jinx, so I'm still on board, at least until I talk to Lily.

"I'll sit on it for a day or two." I look around the large conference room we're in. "Does your boss know that you meet potential investment partners for your side business during your coffee breaks?"

That earns me an unexpected laugh from the twenty-five-year-old. "My dad doesn't give a shit what I do as long as I show up here every day in a suit. One of the perks of working for him is I get to set my schedule. I spend ninety-nine percent of my time developing apps, and the other one percent listening to him bitch about everyone else who works for him."

A decade ago when I was his age, I was breaking my back at a fish market on the Lower East Side during the day and my nights were spent tending bar at a club uptown.

"So I'll see you by the end of the week with the fifty thousand in hand?" Silas pushes back from the table with a sly grin. "The second you fund this, I can take it to the races, Mr. Jones."

I smile at his mention of my surname. The only time he resorts to using it is when he wants more of my money. "You made as much on Jewel Jinx as I did. Why not keep this one to yourself? You can bankroll this on your own."

He tosses his head back and laughs. "Dude, I bought a penthouse and a boat."

It's a rookie mistake and one, I, fortunately, avoided.

"Live and learn, Silas." Standing, I snap my laptop shut and pick it up. "I've lived in the same apartment for twelve years."

"I've been to your place. You live in a shoebox close to midtown."

"I live in a two bedroom apartment that has more than enough room for me."

"I'll give you that." He sets his hand on my shoulder. "You must have thought about moving out of there at some point. Your neighborhood is teeming with tourists."

"I'm not complaining." I face him. "Every corner of this city has its distinct charm, including where I live."

"To each his own." He starts toward the conference room door. "I get the allure of Tribeca. That's why I bought a place there. Nothing could convince me to move to your neck of the woods. I'll never understand what keeps you there, Rocco."

Memories.

They anchor me to that apartment. They always will.

Chapter 3

Dexie

A siren blares as I step out of the Matiz
Cosmetics office tower.

The sound is an integral part of Manhattan.
When I first moved to the city it took me months to
get used to all the noise. It's never quiet, but for the
most part, I've grown to love it.

On days like today, I could do without the
argument that's going on next to me. Two women
are disagreeing about where to go to eat lasagna. I can
tell that they're tourists. The clothing they're wearing
gives them away.

It's the middle of summer and the early
evening temperature is hovering near ninety-five
degrees.

I'm wearing a white sundress with a light pink
cardigan draped over my forearm. They're both
decked out in jeans, white *I heart NY* T-shirts and
black hoodies tied around their waists.

"I didn't mean to overhear your
conversation." I turn toward the women. It's
immediately obvious that they're sisters. "I can make
a great recommendation for pasta."

Both of their faces brighten with broad smiles.

The shorter of the two brunettes speaks first.
"Do you live here?"

I nod. "I do."

The other woman's nose crinkles as her gaze rakes me over. "You look like you belong on the cover of a fashion magazine."

I take the compliment with a smile. I think I look more like I spent my day in a stuffy office going over the marketing materials for the winter launch of Matiz's new lipstick line. The skirt of my dress is wrinkled. My hair is a frizzed mess from the humidity and there's a yellow stain on my cardigan. The deli down the street put too much mustard on my pastrami on rye and the excess dropped on my sweater. I adjust the cardigan to hide the stain, so I don't look like a complete fraud to these two.

I know from experience that a specific question always brightens a tourist's day. "Do you two live here?"

They giggle in unison and their blue eyes narrow in the same way. I suddenly wonder if they resemble their mom or their dad.

The taller of the two women leans closer to me. "We don't live here. We're from Idaho."

"I've never been," I say truthfully. "What's it like?"

They both step to the right to allow a group of people to pass by us. The shorter woman sighs as she looks toward the street and the buses, cars, and delivery trucks creeping along in late afternoon traffic.

"Peaceful," she answers as she points at the woman next to her. "My sister lives closer to the mountains than I do, but I'm not complaining. I love it there."

"It sounds beautiful." I watch as she looks over at her sister. "I hope I can visit someday."

"Where did you buy that?" The taller woman inches closer to me, her gaze pinned on the yellow leather tote that's clutched in my hand. "It's beautiful."

I look down at the bag. It took me weeks to get the design right. I chose this bright color because it symbolizes summer to me. I put the final touches on it right before I moved to my new place. "It's one of mine. I designed it."

They exchange a glance before they both turn back to me. "Do you have a store? A website? Where can we get it?"

Their voices blend as they spit out the questions. I hesitate before I answer. "I can give you my card. I'm only doing custom one-of-a-kind pieces right now."

I fish in my tote for the silver business card holder Sophia gave me for my birthday last year. I tug out two cards and hand one to each woman.

"Can you make that bag in black?" The shorter woman stares down at my card. "I'd love it in black."

"I can do that." I trace my fingertips over the delicate silver chain that runs along the top of the bag. "I can change out any of the details to make it perfect for you."

"I'll email you when I'm back home." She tucks the card into the back pocket of her faded jeans. "I'm Nora Kemp, by the way."

"I'm Dexie Walsh," I say with a smile. "But you knew that from the card."

"I'm Trisha." The other woman nods. "I've been looking for a clutch forever. I've found a few, but I'm still on the hunt for the perfect one. Is that something you can do?"

12

"Absolutely." I pull my phone from my bag and scroll through the photo library until I land on the image of a pink clutch I made last year for a friend of a friend. "Are you thinking of something like this?"

Her eyes scan the screen as her smile spreads quickly. "That's it. I love that, but in white with gold rivets instead of silver and a touch bigger."

"I can work on a sketch and send it to you." I drop my phone back in my tote. "Email me once you're home and we'll collaborate."

"This is fate," Nora says, looking around us. "We were meant to run into you today, Dexie." I'll call it luck because there's the potential for two sales in my future. I know that they may never reach out, but I always hold out hope that the people who show interest in my handbags will follow through and place an order.

"Today would be perfect if we could agree on where to get some pasta." Trisha laughs. "There must be thousands of choices in the city."

"Trust me on this, ladies." I take a step toward the edge of the sidewalk and raise my hand at the approaching traffic. "I'm going to grab us a taxi. You want to eat dinner at Calvetti's."

"Please say you're joining us so you can tell us all about New York," Trisha says, glancing at Nora. "We're here celebrating my fortieth birthday. I'd love to know what it's like to be a twenty-something single gal living in the big city."

It's hard work being a twenty-seven-year-old struggling purse designer who spends her days coming up with catchy campaigns to sell lipstick shades she'll never wear and her nights alone in her bed.

"I assume you're single," Trisha continues. "You're not wearing a ring."

I look down at my bare hands. "I'm still looking for Mr. Right."

"Maybe he's waiting for you at Calevetti's," Nora offers with a sly grin. "Let us buy you dinner as a thank you for breaking up our argument."

Wrapping her arm around her sister's shoulder, Trisha giggles.

"I'd love to, but I have to work on a purse tonight for a client." I smile as a taxi slows. "I'm headed in that direction though. We'll stop at Calvettti's and then I'll walk home and leave you two to enjoy the best pasta in New York City."

Chapter 4

Rocco

Just as I glance toward the windows at the front of my grandmother's restaurant I catch a brief glimpse of long blonde hair kissed with pale pink streaks. The fleeting image is enough to lure me to my feet, but the woman disappears out of sight just as my grandmother approaches with a ten dollar bill in her hand.

"Why are you standing, Rocco?" She waves her hands to motion for me to sit back down. "Your food is coming. Patience, my boy. You need to learn some patience."

I look over at the two women wearing *I heart NY* shirts who just walked in.

My grandmother, Martina Calvetti, adores tourists and native New Yorkers alike. She makes everyone feel at home in her restaurant. The only time I remember her without open arms and a smile on her beautiful face was in the months following my mom's passing.

I was six-years-old, but the memory of my grandma crying as she stood in the kitchen of this restaurant trying to prepare enough food to feed everyone in our family after her eldest daughter's death has stuck with me.

She's not only the strongest woman I've ever known, but she has the biggest heart.

"I thought I saw someone." I don't elaborate beyond that.

The pink-streaked blonde hair was a reminder of the woman who lives in the building next to mine. I caught her eye through the window a few nights ago after dusk fell. She was staring at me. I gladly returned the favor. The next morning I watched as she hurried to get ready for her day.

For the most part, she was in her bathroom out of my view, but as she was leaving her apartment, I saw the light blue dress she was wearing.

I took the stairs two at a time to make it down the six flights before she exited her building.

Her elevator beat me.

When I stepped out of my building, she was already headed down the sidewalk with a pair of red heels on her feet, an orange leather bag slung over her shoulder and her gorgeous hair whipping in the wind.

Physically, she looks nothing like the women I'm typically attracted to, yet there's something about her that I can't shake.

"This is for you." My grandmother drops the ten dollar bill on the table next to my glass of water.

As I sit back down, I look into her blue eyes. They're the same shade as mine. "You're paying me to eat here now? Since when?"

She ruffles my hair. "You need a haircut."

That's debatable. I don't put a lot of thought into my hair. I wash it, towel dry it and it ends up looking unruly. It's working for me judging by the number of second glances I've been getting from women I pass on the sidewalk.

"Marti," I start with the name I've always called her. She's always been Marti to me. She tells me that she christened herself that on the day I was born, so I've never strayed from it. It fits her. Just as the name Rocco suits me. It was my grandfather's first name and I'm proud to be the second Rocco in the family. "I hate to break the news to you, but I can't get a decent haircut for ten dollars."

"Define decent." She twirls her hand in the air. "Anything is better than this."

"Keep your money." I slide the bill back toward her. "I can afford a haircut."

She shakes her head adamantly. Her graying brown hair stays in place in the bun she always pins it into at the base of her neck. "You could use a shave too."

"I didn't come here for the critique. I came for a plate of lasagna."

"You'll eat the spaghetti today."

I laugh loudly. "I ordered the lasagna."

She shoots me a look. "I know what's best for my grandson. You'll eat the spaghetti. I made it myself."

She makes everything herself.

"Spaghetti it is," I acquiesce with a shake of my head.

Her gaze slides to the table where the women wearing the *I heart NY* shirts are now sitting. "I'm going to go over and welcome those two beauties. I'll see if either is available."

"Marti." I rub my temples. "No more set-ups."

"Is it a crime that I want my grandson to have a happy life?" Her hands trail through the air in a wide arc. "Ti amo, ragazzo mio."

I love you, my boy.

The same words my mother would say to me in Italian every night.

"I love you too." I reach for her hand, kissing her calloused palm. "I have a happy life. You're a big part of that."

She pats me on the top of the head. "Use the money to get a haircut. You'll attract more women if you clean yourself up."

I laugh as Manuel, one of the servers, approaches with a round white plate piled high with spaghetti and meatballs.

I'm eager to eat and then head home. With any luck, the beautiful woman who lives in the building next to mine will be waiting for me by her window tonight.

Chapter 5

Dexie

I bang my fist against the cover of the air conditioner again. It starts up with a thud and a whir, but it's short-lived. It sputters, just like it did the first two times I tried the novel approach of punching it to get it to work.

It's unbearably hot in here. I felt the stifling heat the moment I walked in and hit the switch to turn on the track lighting on the ceiling. By the time I shut my apartment door, my dress was on the floor and I was on my way to take a quick cool shower.

I put on a pair of black yoga shorts and a matching sports bra after I toweled off. My lack of clothing should bring me some relief, but it doesn't.

Sighing, I type out a text to the building's superintendent, Harold, again. It's the third one I've sent in the two hours since I got home.

I tell him that my skin feels like it's melting off and I need him to come to my apartment now.

I press send even though I doubt he'll reply. He hasn't responded to the first two texts or the voicemail I left him.

I'm not surprised. I heard a loud thud come from the apartment across the hall from mine ten minutes ago. Maybe their air conditioner died too.

I take another long sip of cold water from the glass I've refilled twice before I set it back down on a small table next to the worn red wingback chair in the corner.

Hydration is my only ally right now.

My phone vibrates in my hand. My gaze drops, my heart leaping with the hope that it's Harold.

"Dammit," I mutter under my breath when I see the text is from Sophia.

Sophia: *What are you doing right now?*

It's typical Sophia. She sends the same text whenever she wants to meet for a drink or dinner. Since I already ate a piece of pizza on the go on my way home, and I'm not in the mood for a martini, I cut to the chase to save us both time.

Dexie: *I'm in my hot as hell apartment wearing almost nothing. I can't hang out tonight. I need to work.*

The dots on the screen start jumping while she types a response.

Sophia: *Why is it hot as hell? You have an air conditioner. Turn it on before you pass out.*

I laugh at her predictability. Sophia is the most caring person I've ever met. Since she became a mom, her need to nurture everyone around her has increased tenfold.

Dexie: *Before you tell me to call the super, I have. The air conditioner isn't working.*

I smile knowing that she's about to invite me to her apartment. She has a guest room that overlooks Central Park. I crashed there once when we had too much red wine on her birthday.

Her husband, Nicholas, made me feel like I was a member of the family. They've both always treated me with nothing but love and respect.

Sophia: *Come stay here tonight. We can hang out. I'll help you with your work. We'll have some wine.*

I laugh aloud, my fingers flying over the screen of my phone.

Dexie: *You're the best, but I'm staying here. I can deal with the heat.*

I finish what's left of the water in my glass while she types.

Sophia: *The offer is open if you change your mind, but do me one favor.*

I start toward my kitchen faucet to refill my glass, but I stop mid-step when I look out one of the windows and catch a glimpse of the building next door.

He's back.

The man from last night is standing in front of his window, wearing a T-shirt and jeans.

My phone buzzes in my hand, so I drop my gaze to it just long enough to read Sophia's next message.

Sophia: *You said you're wearing next to nothing so unless you have something covering your windows, you need something to cover you. Put on a robe or some clothes before your neighbors see you!*

I smile to myself as I type out a response.

Dexie: *Too late. I need to go.*

My phone is only silent for a few seconds before it starts to ring. I toss it on the bed, knowing that Sophia's curiosity and imagination are both getting the better of her.

She'd never let a stranger see her this exposed.

Normally, I wouldn't either, but the way the man next door is staring at me makes me want to twirl in place to give him a glimpse of every angle of my body.

My phone quiets briefly before it starts up again, the jarring sound of the ringer suddenly overshadowed by a loud knock at my door.

"Ms. Walsh, it's Harold."

My gaze darts back to the man at the window. His arms are crossed over his chest. His eyes are pinned to my every move.

I'm tempted to tell Harold to come back tomorrow, but the air in my apartment is too hot and stuffy for me to work or sleep.

I race to the clothing rack in the corner. I yank off the first thing my hand lands on.

It's a man's white dress shirt I picked up on sale last winter to wear with one of my favorite skirts. I wrap it around me, buttoning it as I call out, "I'm coming."

Once I swing open the door, I turn back to look at the window, but my gorgeous neighbor has vanished, along with the hope I had that I'd get to see more of him tonight.

Chapter 6

Rocco

I take my time in the shower, trusting that when I'm done, Harold Demarco will be long gone.

He interrupted a moment between my almost nude neighbor and me thirty minutes ago.

I caught a brief glimpse of her in a bra and yoga shorts before she draped what looked like a man's dress shirt over her body.

I haven't seen a guy in her apartment, so I'm assuming the shirt belongs to her. I'm hoping like hell it does.

The apartment she lives in has been devoid of blinds for more than a year. I stopped glancing in that direction after I saw a man fucking a redheaded woman against one of the windows months ago.

I locked eyes with her, she tempted me with a finger curl to join them and I declined with a shake of my head.

When I'm with a woman, I want her all to myself. I don't share.

Stepping out of the shower stall, I wrap a white towel around my waist. Pushing my hair back from my forehead I walk into the main living space.

A quick glance at the window rewards me with the sight of my neighbor standing with her back to me, the dress shirt still covering every inch of her skin except for her toned legs.

Harold is next to her, a phone against his ear as he shakes his head.

The blonde beauty lives in a dump. The building should have been condemned years ago, but the owner orders Harold to patch the problems whenever he's forced to so he can keep the inspectors at bay.

I've watched dozens of tenants come and go from my perch across the street. The walls in the apartment I'm staring into have thousands of stories to tell, but none as interesting as the one I'm watching now.

Harold is on the move. He crosses the apartment headed straight for the door.

My pulse leaps, my cock hardening at the thought of my neighbor being alone again.

"Fuck," falls from my lips when Harold swings open the door and a woman is standing there. She's average height with brown hair bobbing around her shoulders.

She pushes her way past him and approaches the blonde.

Words are exchanged between the three of them before the brunette grabs a pair of jeans hung over the back of a chair and shoves them into my neighbor's hands.

I watch as she walks toward the bathroom with even steps, the pink streaks in her hair catching the overhead light.

Whatever moment we might have had has been lost.

I turn away from the window, rub my hand over my erection and close my eyes.

I'll get off tonight to the fleeting image I have stored in my mind of her body in that bra and those shorts.

I crave more. I want to see more of her, know more about her and touch all of her.

Tonight I'll have to settle for less.

***

"Look what the cat dragged in," Lenore Halston calls back over her shoulder. "Rocco is here at the crack of dawn."

She's not lying. It's early.

I barely slept last night.

After I pulled on a pair of black boxer briefs and jeans, I stood at the window and watched my neighbor leave with the brunette woman.

By the time I went to bed hours later, she hadn't returned.

I woke with a start just after four a.m. and couldn't help but notice that the overhead lights were still on in the apartment across from mine.

The bed was empty.

I went back to my bed, tossed and turned for an hour and then hit the pavement for a run.

Another quick shower and a cup of coffee were followed by a subway ride here.

Looking polished in a three-piece gray suit, Glenn Halston appears around a corner in the luxurious office he keeps on Park Avenue to feed his ego.

The man is worth as much as I am. He put his life savings in tech stocks before smartphones hit it big. He's been a mentor of sorts to me for years, helping me navigate the world of investing in other people's dream businesses.

He pushes his black-rimmed eyeglasses up the bridge of his nose. "You don't come bearing gifts?"

I laugh aloud. "My presence isn't enough?"

"It is for me," Lenore, his wife, fans herself with a piece of paper as she looks over the black V-neck T-shirt and jeans I'm wearing. "You're as handsome as ever, Rocco."

"Compliments are the key to this man's heart." I tap my hand over the center of my chest.

"Enough with the flirting with my wife." Glenn chuckles. "I'm not missing something here, am I? We don't have a meeting planned for today."

We don't, but I want his take on the app Silas ran past me. I made a promise to Glenn that I would give him a shot at investing in Silas's next venture after the success of Jewel Jinx.

I spoke to Lilly Parker on the phone about the app yesterday afternoon. She told me to jump in with both feet and she wants a percentage of the action too. I'm here to give Glenn the option of doing the same.

"I have an opportunity you might be interested in," I say, resting an elbow on the reception desk.

He leans closer, his blue eyes intense. "Should we bring Rhoda in on this?"

Rhoda McCullough, the third in our trio of angel investors, has zero interest in anything tech related. Initially, I thought that was because of her age. The woman is a breathtaking seventy-year-old with a penchant for the finer things in life and younger men. Her current husband is just shy of fifty-five.

"It's not in her wheelhouse," I explain.

He glances over at his wife before his gaze lands on me again. "Rhoda has a few new prospects. She wants us to set up something for them next week. Do you have time for that?"

It's what Rhoda lives for. She lines up a handful of people looking to launch their start-ups. They pitch their ideas to the three of us. If any of us see potential, an offer may be made to invest in their products, their companies or sometimes their visions.

I used to enjoy those sessions more than I do now, but that's how Silas landed in my life, so I won't turn my back on potential.

"I'm in."

"Lenore will gather the info and send you an email." He tosses his wife a wink. "Come on back to my office and give me the details on the opportunity that brought you here this early."

The only thing that brought me here this early was my reluctance to stay in my apartment a minute longer. The four walls offer me comfort most of the time, but some mornings, like today, the silence is deafening.

Chapter 7

Dexie

I study the bag slung over the shoulder of one of my favorite people in the world. Mabel Husher burst into my life four months ago.

She grabbed hold of my purse on the subway. I had my hand in the air to push her off of me before I was turned around.

When I realized it was a petite, gray-haired diva gripping the leather strap, I calmed the hell down.

All she wanted was a closer look at the navy blue handbag I was carrying and the name of the designer.

I handed her my card, and since that day she's bought three custom pieces from me, including the soft gray leather tote that I'm staring at now.

I'm the worst when it comes to critiquing my handiwork. I always find a small flaw whenever I revisit a bag I worked on in the past. In the case of Mabel's gray tote, I spot the end of a loose thread dangling near the base of one of the straps.

"I didn't expect to see you today, Mabel." I step aside to allow a group of my co-workers to board the elevator that leads up to the Matiz Cosmetics corporate offices.

I'm on my lunch break and since I didn't have time to pack a sandwich at home, I need to grab something quick that will hold me over until quitting time.

I stayed at Sophia's penthouse last night after she showed up and dragged me from my ninety plus degree apartment.

I would have been more than happy to spend the night staring at my neighbor, but Sophia was insistent that I go home with her.

By the time I got back to my apartment this morning, the air conditioner was working and my handsome neighbor was nowhere in sight.

"I was on my way to your office to see you." Mabel looks me over. "I don't know how you get away with pairing a red dress with purple shoes and a yellow bag, but it works on you."

It does work.

I once bought into the idea that fashion has to follow a prescribed path, but those days are over. My style is as unique as I am and I like it that way.

Mabel is wearing a sleek black dress and matching shoes. The brief glimpse of a red sole that I spotted as I stepped off the elevator wasn't surprising.

It's only ever the best for Mabel, which is why I'm still shocked that she carries my bags around Manhattan paired with her designer clothes and shoes.

I take her compliment with a smile. "What can I help you with?"

I'm hoping it's another new bag. Mabel has never balked at the price I've charged her. It's expensive, but she's the one who told me that my talent was priceless.

"Can we sit?" She gestures at a fabric-covered bench across the lobby.

My stomach grumbles a response, but I ignore it. "Of course."

I follow closely behind her, taking note of the slight limp in her gait. I have no idea how old she is, but I do know that she gets around Manhattan with the same precision and speed as someone my age.

I settle in next to her on the bench, running my fingertip around the edge of a fading brown stain on the off-white twill fabric. It was a drip from a cup of coffee in my hand months ago that blemished the otherwise pristine cushion.

She turns to face me. The large diamond on her ring finger catches the light as she folds her hands in her lap. "Did I ever mention my sister to you?"

I try to hide the frown on my lips. This isn't a promising way to open a discussion about a new handbag, but I go with it because Mabel has been good to me. "No, you haven't."

"Her name is Rhoda." She rolls her green eyes. "She's older than me but insists she's younger. I swear she'd have her birth certificate changed if they'd let her."

I bite back a laugh, hoping that she's segueing into a purse order for her sister.

"Rhoda has the brains." She runs a red manicured fingernail over her chin. "I have the beauty."

I nod, knowing that she's teasing. She told me soon after we met that she loved her career as the Chief Financial Officer of an energy company before she retired last year.

"Rhoda does this thing." Leaning closer, she lowers her voice to a whisper. "She helps people like you."

Like me?

I try not to look offended since I don't know what she's talking about, although if I had to hedge a guess, I'd say it's about the way I'm dressed. I'm basing that on the fact that she's looking me over from head-to-toe.

Maybe that compliment she just threw my way wasn't genuine after all.

The majority of the clothing I wear is from Sophia's line, Ella Kara. It's affordable enough for everyone, including me even though I rarely pay for any of it.

Sophia uses me as a test model. She creates a new design, gives me her handmade sample and sends me out into the world to gather feedback.

I never complain. How can I when I spend next to nothing on my wardrobe?

She almost always has one of my bags in her hand, and I regularly wear her clothing designs.

It's a fashion win for both of us.

Mabel picks up the gray tote and swings it in a tight circle. "I showed her this yesterday. She wants to meet you."

Maybe there is a purse order in my immediate future.

I shove a hand in my bag to fish for my business card holder. "I'll grab one of my cards. You can give it to her or I can take her number and call her."

Mabel swats my knee. "I've already given her your name, your number and I showed her that website you have."

My stomach growls a reminder that my lunch break is ticking away, so I inch our discussion forward. "Is Rhoda looking for a bag?"

"Heavens no." Her eyes scan my face. "She wants you to meet with her and her investor friends to discuss the future of your company."

Holy hell.

I stare at her pink stained lips, playing her words over and over again in my head.

"Someone will reach out to you soon with the details, but I wanted to tell you the good news face-to-face." She sighs. "Show them your best work. If you do that, you'll be sure to seal a deal."

I nod, my mind racing with mental images of all my recent designs. "I'll do that."

"I'll check in again once the meeting is over." She looks down at the tote. "If I could, I'd partner with you, but my husband and I have everything tied up right now."

"I... I...Mabel I can't thank you enough for this."

"I told you the day we met that you'd go places." She glides to her feet. "This is your ticket to that place, Dexie."

She's right. I've wanted to find a business partner for the past two years, but no one other than Sophia has shown any interest.

I was touched when she offered her money in exchange for equity in my company, but our friendship is too important to me to risk losing it over a business disagreement, so I declined with a smile and an appreciative hug.

This is different. This is a legitimate investor who can help catapult my purse business to the next level.

"Look at the time. I have to run." Mabel gives me a brief hug before she sets off toward the lobby doors.

I glance down at my phone. I have a marketing meeting I need to get to in fifteen minutes. It leaves no time for lunch, but I'd trade food for a future any day of the week.

Chapter 8

Rocco

As soon as I close my apartment door behind me, I toss my phone and keys on a leather chair in the corner.

I head straight for the window that overlooks my neighbor's apartment. It's early evening and she's home.

I spot her immediately. She's standing next to her bed.

Tonight she's dressed in a white tank top and faded cut-off denim shorts. Her hair is piled high on her head. Several blonde and pink strands have fallen loose and are playing against the side of her face.

She's lost in thought. Her gaze is trained on an array of handbags on display on her bed.

I take a seat next to the window. It affords me a clear view of every one of her movements, including the intermittent shaking of her head whenever she picks up a bag before placing it down again.

Maybe she's choosing one as an accessory for an outfit she's planning on wearing tonight.

The thought makes my stomach roll.

I don't know the woman's name, or her relationship status but the thought of her giving her attention to another man sparks a shot of envy within me.

She tosses a pink bag onto the bed before she turns her back to me.

I get a perfect view of her gorgeous ass.

It's round and plump. The shorts she's wearing strain to contain her generous curves.

I move to accommodate my growing erection.

My jeans feel too tight. I want to palm my cock. The idea of stroking it while watching her is tempting.

She spins on her heel and faces the window.

Her ample tits lift under her tank top as she takes in a quick breath.

I've thought about her nipples, wondered what color they are, how hard they get when sucked and what sounds she'll make when my teeth close around them.

When.

It's not a question of if I'll fuck her, but when.

I saw the way she was staring at me the other night. The woman wants me as desperately as I want her.

I rise to my feet and lean my hands against the window, willing the beauty to look up at me.

My breath rushes over the glass with each of my labored exhales. Every beat of my heart is a beacon she can't hear.

I want her to feel my presence.

Her chin lifts and that's when it happens. Her dark eyes latch onto mine and a sweet, slow smile spreads over her full lips.

***

Her phone interrupted us briefly.

She looked at it twice before she finally reached over and picked it up from the bed.

I wish to fuck I could read lips.

I want to know what her name is and what she was saying to the person on the other end of the call. I want to know what they were saying to her that brought an even broader grin to her face.

Hell, more than anything I want to hear her voice.

In my mind, it's husky and sexy. Her laugh must be intoxicating.

She throws the phone back on the bed and squares her attention on me again.

I know what I want so I take the lead in our silent interaction.

I slide the T-shirt I'm wearing over my head.

Her eyes widen when I take a step back to give her a good look at my upper body. I take care of myself. I need to. There are too many people in this world who depend on me.

When her eyes finally trail back up to my face, I tilt my chin forward in a challenge.

I want her shirt off.

She points at her tank top. Her brows rise in question.

I scratch my chin and nod.

Her gaze darts over my building. I have no idea how many eyes are pinned to her right now.

This is Manhattan. Most New Yorkers don't pay close attention to anything their neighbors are doing, but when they look like the blonde beauty I'm staring at, it's impossible not to be transfixed.

I wait for her to shake her head in protest, but that's not what happens.

Her hands fall to the bottom hem of her shirt and she slides it up slowly. It's so fucking leisurely that it feels like time has almost stopped.

Every inch of her stomach is exposed before she stops with the fabric bunched under her tits.

I know she's wearing a bra. I saw the pink strap slip down from her shoulder when she was tossing a bag onto her bed.

With a sly smile, the shirt is up and over her head.

I move so near to the window that my lips almost touch the glass. She feels so close, yet she's so far away. It's too goddamn far away.

When her arms cross over the pale pink bra, I slap my palm against the window and shake my head.

She can't hear anything; not the sound of my hand hitting the glass or the pounding beat of my heart.

It's racing.

The need to touch her is strong.

Her hands move slowly, trailing over the fabric of her bra until they land on her stomach.

I want her to reach back and unhook the clasp on the bra. I want to see more.

Her gaze drops to her body and she shivers. When she looks up, her eyes lock on mine. I fight the urge to turn and run.

It wouldn't take me more than five minutes to race out of my place and be at her apartment door.

I raise my hand to my chest, pat it twice and point at her.

She understands my silent invitation to join her, but the faint shake of her head is enough to keep me in place.

She's not ready for more. *Yet.*

Fortunately, I'm a very patient man.

Chapter 9

Dexie

I turned him down last night.

I don't know why I didn't wave my hot-as-sin neighbor over when he gestured that he wanted to join me in my apartment.

After the regrettable shake of my head, he nodded at me and was about to turn away when I blew him a kiss.

It was an impulsive, sophomoric thing to do, but it did bring a smile to his face.

Once he moved to turn off the light in his apartment, I leaned against the window and cursed myself for not taking the plunge.

I'm doing it again now.

I woke up ten minutes ago, and the first thing I did was leap out of bed and dart for my window.

The hope that I had that he'd be standing there, shirtless with a cup of coffee in his hand, and another invitation to join me was quickly replaced with disappointment.

I sigh heavily before I turn around and face my apartment.

Handbags are everywhere. There are a few still on my bed. I pushed those aside before I went to sleep. Four of them are on the kitchen counter. They're in my "*maybe*" pile.

I'm no closer to deciding which purses to show the potential investors than I was last night.

A soft knock at my apartment door draws my gaze up.

Could it be? Is it possible that my neighbor decided to show up on my doorstep unannounced?

I run my hands through my hair and look down at what I'm wearing.

After I took a shower last night, I slipped into a pair of pink panties and a black T-shirt.

Another series of raps on my door lures me closer. I take a few tentative steps before I call out, "Who is it?"

I want to know his name. I ache to know the name of the man who was staring at me last night.

"It's me."

My hope deflates at the sound of Sophia's voice on the other side of the door.

"Sophia?" I ask for no reason other than to give me enough time to yank on a pair of cut-off jean shorts over my panties.

"I have coffee and those banana chocolate chip muffins you love," she singsongs. "Open the door, Dex."

I rub my hands over my face. As much as I hate to admit it, I'm glad she's here. I need help choosing which handbags I'll show the potential investors.

That has to be my priority today even though all I want to do is spend this Saturday sitting on the windowsill staring into the apartment across from mine.

***

Hours later, as I enter my apartment after having dinner with Sophia, my mind is racing.

I took a call thirty minutes ago from a woman named Lenore Halston. She apologized for bothering me on a Saturday evening before she explained that she was reaching out on behalf of a group of angel investors.

My hand shook as I held the phone to my ear and stared down at the linen tablecloth. I couldn't look across the table at Sophia because I knew that I'd tear up.

We'd spent all day talking about all the *what if* possibilities.

I'll get my chance to pitch my handbag design business in less than a week to a group of strangers. One of them may change my future.

I glance over at the six purses that Sophia and I chose earlier. I needed her expert eye to help me wade through the sea of emotions I was feeling. She's objective and explained the reasoning behind each of her suggestions. I agreed with two, but ultimately picked the ones that I feel best represent my brand.

In just a few days, I'll show those designs to the investors. With any luck, I'll leave that meeting with a business partner.

I walk over to the lamp and turn it on. It's early evening, but it's been overcast all day. The low hanging clouds have stolen all the natural light from this space.

A clap of thunder draws my gaze to the windows.

Time stops when I look over at the building next to mine.

He's there, standing in the window as rain beats down on the city.

I stare at his face before my gaze drops to his muscular chest and the white towel wrapped around his waist.

He must have just showered. I can't tell from where I'm standing if his hair is wet or not. It's pushed back from his forehead.

I wonder what his hair feels like, what his skin smells like.

I look at his lips and wish, more than anything that I knew what it feels like to kiss him.

His hand drops to his waist and the top of the towel.

"Drop it," I whisper against the glass. "Please, drop it."

His hand trails up his toned stomach to his chest before it lands on his chin.

My eyes meet his again. He smiles in a devilish way that tells me that he wants more from me.

I understand. I've watched him often enough that I recognize the subtle nuances in the way he looks at me. I see the fevered desire that is there in his eyes.

I drop my hands to the front of my short pink sundress.

I unbutton it, taking my time to reveal the pink lace bra and panties that I put on earlier.

His head is slowly bobbing up and down when I reach the last pink pearl button. My lingerie is sheer. When I open the dress, he'll see everything.

I hesitate briefly, not because I don't want this man to see my body, but because I know, full well, that other eyes may be on me.

I scan the building looking for any shadowy figures standing near windows, but I don't see another soul.

When my gaze meets his again, I start to open my dress, confident that he'll want to come over. I'll agree this time.

I crave this man's touch, even if I don't know anything about him other than what he looks like.

His expression shifts as the front of my dress parts. I study his every movement, waiting for him to show me, with his body, that he wants me as much as I want him.

I stop breathing when he glances over his shoulder.

His head drops, his hand fists against the glass and when he finally looks up at me, I see defeat where I want to see desire.

He mouths something to me that I can't make out since I'm too busy wrapping my dress back around me.

I watch in silence as he moves away from the window and disappears around a corner.

I take a step back in an effort to retreat from the vulnerability I'm feeling.

When he appears again, there's a dark haired woman in a white one-shoulder jumpsuit next to him. Her hands are wrapped around his bicep, her gaze pinned to his handsome face.

He glances my way briefly, but I move out of view.

I can't watch him with another woman. I turn my back to both of them and button up my dress before I grab my keys and purse and head straight out my door.

Chapter 10

Rocco

I curse under my breath as I watch my beautiful neighbor bolt from her apartment.

I know exactly why she's headed out into the rain. She made an assumption about the brunette standing next to me.

There's no way the woman who was undressing for me could know that my unexpected visitor is my cousin.

Gina Calvetti has an uncanny ability to show up at my apartment at the worst possible time.

I'm pissed off, but I fight the urge to express that. Instead, I reach for Gina's hand and give it a slight squeeze. "I'm going to put on a pair of jeans and a T-shirt."

She lets go of my arm. The fact that I'm only wearing a towel didn't register with Gina when I opened my apartment door. She dove into a one-sided conversation about her ex-boyfriend and his wife as she led me into my living room.

Gina looks to me for relationship advice. She has yet to realize that I've never offered any words of wisdom related to the men she's been involved with. It's not that I don't have an opinion. I do. Gina is like a sister to me, but she never lets me get a word in.

"Hurry," she says, tapping her foot against the floor. "Do you want to get something to eat?"

"Sure." I'd ask what she's in the mood for, but our grandmother would see it as a betrayal if we went anywhere but Calvetti's.

I have no problem sitting down for a meal at any one of the thousands of other restaurants in Manhattan, but Gina's loyalty to the family is unwavering.

Guilt will haunt her if we hit up the French restaurant I recently invested in. I'm a fan of the food and the head chef, Lucien, but Gina won't make it through the appetizer course before she's on the phone with Marti confessing her culinary sin.

"I'll order an Uber," she mutters under her breath as I walk toward my bedroom. "I have so much to tell you, Rocco."

I'm sure she does. Gina's never been short of words.

I'll sit with her and eat a plate of my grandmother's pasta while I listen to her complain about her life. The entire time I'll be thinking about the briefest glimpse of my neighbor's body that I caught before the promise of more was stolen from me.

***

"Do you know her?"

I turn back to look at Gina. She's sitting across the table from me, her hand wrapped around a glass of expensive red wine.

She knows that Marti will foot the bill for this dinner, so she's indulging.

I'll even the scales by sending a bouquet of pale pink peonies to the restaurant tomorrow afternoon. They're Marti's favorite and never fail to bring a smile to her face.

"Do I know who?" I question.

Gina rolls her eyes. "You keep looking over your shoulder at that woman with pink hair. Who is she?"

She's not who I want her to be.

I caught a glimpse of her pink-streaked blonde hair when we walked in. As tempting as it was to march over to the table she's sharing with a guy in a suit, I resisted.

I greeted Marti with a kiss on her cheek, sat my ass down in a chair next to the table she directed us to and then turned to see if I could get a good look at the woman's face even though her back is to me.

It took three glances over my shoulder before I finally caught sight of her profile.

She's not my neighbor. This woman isn't nearly as beautiful as the one who was undressing for me in front of her window earlier.

"I don't know her," I answer truthfully.

"You want to know her," Gina counters with a smile.

I shake my head. "Not her."

"Look at you acting all cagey." She takes a sip of the wine, closing her dark brown eyes to savor the taste.

I ignore the comment. Most of my time spent with Gina is devoted to watching her put on a brave face in the aftermath of a break-up. She reaches out when her heart has taken a beating.

"You're too good for him, Gina."

She sets the glass down. "You always say that. It never helps."

I heard about her ex and his new bride on the way here. He proposed to the woman he started dating after he dumped my cousin. They walked down the aisle earlier today, which is why Gina showed up at my place.

"Time helps." I reach for her hand and squeeze it." You'll find the right guy for you."

She looks down at our hands. "Do you think you'll ever find the right girl for you?"

It's a topic I'll skip.

"I made you both the tortellini." Marti appears next to the table with a server by her side. Two large white bowls of pasta are in his hands.

"I ordered the ravioli, Grandma." Gina smiles up at Marti.

"You'll eat the tortellini," Marti quips as the server places the bowls down in front of us. "I made it myself. Now eat."

Chapter 11

Dexie

"You're going to walk out of that meeting this afternoon with a new business partner." Sophia adjusts the collar of my dress. "I am telling you, Dex. Today is a day that will go down in history."

I wouldn't go that far.

I know she means well, but spending every evening with Sophia this week has started to wear on me.

Her help with preparing my pitch for the potential investors has been vital. I'll never be able to repay her for the time she's devoted to this.

I've stolen moments away from her husband, Nicholas, and her daughter, Winter. I had dinner with all of them the past three nights. Sophia insisted so that we could get to work as soon as she finished reading Winter her bedtime stories.

I turned her down when she offered her spare bedroom to me. She didn't want me going home late every night. In her mind, I'd be safer tucked in the bed down the hall from her.

I admit I was tempted, and not just because the bed is a dream to sleep in. I didn't want to get home and look out my window to see the man I've been fantasizing about with someone else.

I was disappointed when I saw the beautiful dark-haired woman with my half-naked neighbor. I had no right to be since I've never met the man and we don't share anything but a direct view into each other's apartments.

I went to a movie the night I saw them together. By the time I got home, his apartment was dark. I have no idea if that meant he'd left or if he was rolling around in bed with her behind a closed door.

I was too tired to care.

I crawled between the sheets in my bed, fell fast asleep and woke up with a text invitation to brunch with Sophia.

Since then, my life has been split between my work at Matiz and preparing for the meeting this afternoon with the trio of potential backers for my business.

"You look amazing." Sophia picks a piece of lint from the front of the black dress she designed for me.

It's elegant and understated. A vertical line of white buttons dots the front of the dress, leading up to a white collar.

It's cinched at my waist with a thin white leather belt. The strappy high-heeled black sandals on my feet are new. I bought them after work yesterday, even though I have a pair of red heels that I think would complement the dress perfectly.

When I ran my footwear choice by Sophia, she insisted that I tone it down.

"Let the bags shine, Dex."

Those were her words. I took them to heart, which is why my pinky toes feel like they're about to be pinched right off my feet by the hard leather straps.

I brush a strand of wayward hair back from my face.

The soft sigh that escapes Sophia says more than any words ever could.

She's been trying to persuade me for days to dye the pink streaks in my hair blonde. She even went so far as to book me an appointment with her hair stylist after work yesterday. I canceled it and assured her that I'd smooth into a bun for the meeting.

She balked, but when I told her that it was my hair, and the pink wasn't going anywhere, she shrugged her shoulders and muttered under her breath that she hoped it wouldn't ruin my chances of landing a deal.

It's pinned on top of my head in a messy bun at the moment, and that's the way it will stay.

"You have everything you need, right?" She asks expectantly, her gaze dropping to the designer rolling suitcase by my side.

It belongs to her. The six handbags that I'm bringing to the pitch are tucked in there, along with my red shoes. I slid those in for back up before Sophia arrived at my apartment this morning.

I was up before dawn broke, sitting on my windowsill with a cup of coffee in my hand and a stomach filled with butterflies.

"I'm ready," I say semi-confidently. "I should leave soon."

Lenore Halston called me yesterday to confirm the place and time. I told her I'd be there early. Unless I leave now, I'll have to eat those words.

"Be yourself." Sophia stands back and looks me over from head to foot. "I'm proud of you, Dex."

They're words that I've rarely heard in my life, so they shoot straight to my heart. I blow out a breath to keep myself from getting overly emotional.

"I'll call you as soon as the meeting is over," I promise as I reach for the handle of the suitcase. "Are you going to work now?"

"Not a chance." She laughs, brushing a hand over the front of her yellow sundress. "I followed your lead. I took the day off. A late lunch at Nova is the only thing on my calendar for the afternoon."

The significance of that isn't lost on me.

Nova is our go-to restaurant for celebrating anything and everything. We only eat there when something monumental has happened to one of us. Her confidence in me is humbling.

"This is it." I reach for the doorknob, glancing back at the windows that overlook the building next door.

As much as I wish the mystery man would appear, my future is on the line and I have to stay focused. I'm on a mission to secure a partner for my business and nothing is more important than that.

Chapter 12

Rocco

I'm a lucky bastard.

I know it. The two people seated on either side of me know it too.

I just locked down a potential deal with the owner of a dog-grooming product.

Pets aren't part of my day-to-day life. I can't keep a plant alive in my apartment, so I have no place taking on the care of a dog, cat or even a goldfish.

Benefitting from the devotion others have to their pets is my place. I fought hard with Rhoda to land the deal, but ultimately my offer to take the product to a contact that is the purchasing manager of a nationwide pet store tipped the scales in my direction.

"How many more?" Glenn whispers under his breath.

Lenore glances at the closed door before her gaze drops to a sheet of paper in her hands.

We generally do this at Glenn's office, but today is an exception.

Lenore invited more than twenty people to attend this session.

That's why we're in a rented space on Park Avenue with a waiting room that's three times the size of this conference room.

"He was the seventeenth, so only three more," Lenore says. "You have a five-minute potty break if you need it."

I don't need it, but I could use a leg stretch.

I push back from the table, adjusting the buckle of the black belt I'm wearing. I put on gray slacks and a white button-down shirt this morning. I rolled the sleeves of the shirt up to my elbows two hours ago.

Whenever we head into the homestretch of these sessions, I get restless.

Most of my days are spent on the move, visiting the offices and businesses of the people I've partnered with. Being in one place for endless hours isn't interesting to me.

I'm ready to call it a day and leave Glenn and Rhoda to consider the next three pitches on their own, but I'll kick my own ass if I miss out on something promising.

"Where do you think you're going, handsome?" Rhoda's hand lands on my arm.

I pat her fingers gently. "Not far. I need to take a walk."

"I'll come." She stands in a rush. "I don't want you influencing the people who are still waiting with your charm and good looks."

I laugh aloud. "I promise I'll keep my eyes on you, Rhoda, if you do the same."

She gives me the once over. "That's a promise I'll gladly keep."

"I'm coming too," Glenn pipes up. "I don't want anyone having an advantage over me when it comes to the last three pitches."

***

I kept up my end of the bargain when we left the conference room. I only glanced briefly at the people preparing to present their proposals to us.

Lenore said there were only three pitches left, but the waiting room was packed with a group of at least two dozen men and women wearing bright orange T-shirts.

Rhoda stopped to talk to someone she recognized, but I kept my head down. I hit the coffee room to grab a bottle of water before I circled back and headed straight into the conference room.

Lenore tried to convince me to eat one of the sandwiches she had brought in hours earlier, but I passed.

I'll finish this out and then drop by Calvetti's to see Marti. A plate of pasta will be in front of me ten minutes after I arrive there.

I watch as the group wearing the eye-searing neon orange shirts file in. They're carrying camping equipment which means Rhoda is the only one who is going to find this interesting. Her connection to the leader of the pack, a guy in his early twenties with bright blue eyes and a grin from ear-to-ear, guarantees that they have a good shot of leaving here with her on board.

Rhoda invests from the heart. If a pitch sparks emotion in her, she'll pursue a deal even if they don't always work out once her financial advisor has had a chance to look at the numbers.

I try to zone out the long-winded pitch about a new brand of camping gear designed to fit in the back of a compact car.

I keep my eyes trained on the blond-haired guy who is enthusiastically listing off the benefits of getting into the great outdoors and out of the confines of Manhattan.

"The buildings in this city are so close together you can practically touch your neighbors," he spouts to a chorus of laughter from his colleagues.

My mind wanders to the other night and the beauty that lives in the apartment across from mine. I haven't spotted her since, although much of my time this week has been focused on getting a deal locked in with Silas.

The bar around the corner from his office is where he prefers to conduct business, so I met him there two nights ago and again last night. He tried to convince me to accept a smaller equity percentage in Word Wize in exchange for a higher share in the new app idea he's already working on.

It was a hard pass.

I kept my eye on my watch the entire time I was with him. I wanted out of the bar so I could get home to my window and the woman next door.

I rake my fingers through my hair. Just thinking about my beautiful neighbor's body sets off a firestorm inside of me.

If she's there when I get home tonight, I'm going to make it clear to her that I want our exchanges to progress from searing gazes through glass to my hands on her body.

"I'm in," Rhoda announces in the middle of the guy's pitch. "I love it. I'll give you exactly what you're asking."

I hear the audible sigh of relief from Glenn as I breathe out one of my own.

Two more presentations to sit through and I'll be free.

Chapter 13

Dexie

Last.

I'm the very last person to enter that conference room.

I've been sitting in this waiting room for hours watching person after person walk through that door to face the trio of investors on the other side.

Some exited with smiles on their faces, a few were in tears. It was obvious that there was no joy attached to those.

The large group of people who went in thirty minutes ago came out high-fiving each other. They got a deal.

Right now, a woman a few years older than me is behind the closed door trying to convince at least one of the people with the big bank accounts to partner with her in an organic soap business.

I listened while she rehearsed her pitch.

It was good, so good.

She obviously took hours to polish her presentation.

I did too, but the lump in my throat is telling me that I should have invested more time into preparing for this.

I feel a mix of anxiety and regret, but I push it aside when I take a deep breath.

"You're going to do great, Ms. Walsh."

I look up to where Lenore Halston is standing next to the closed door of the conference room. She's been in and out of there all afternoon.

I smile in response.

"I promise that none of them bite," she says softly. "Can I get you anything? There's a coffee room down the hall. I'm about to head down there to grab myself a bottle of water."

It was the one thing I forgot to slide into my purse before I left home.

I'd taken the time to fill up my travel water bottle and put it in the fridge last night so it would be chilled before I came here, but of course, it slipped my mind.

"You wouldn't mind grabbing one for me too, would you?" I sigh, licking my lower lip. "I'm parched."

"Consider it done," she says, glancing over at the closed door of the conference room. "I'll be back in a jiffy."

I nod, even though I have no idea how long a *jiffy* is. All I hope for is that she rounds the waiting room corner with that water before I have to present my idea to the investors.

Too-tight shoes and a dry mouth are not going to help me land a deal.

I suck in a breath and stare down at my now-swollen feet. The straps of the sandals have been cutting into my flesh all afternoon.

I got up three times and walked down the corridor to the ladies' room in the hope that the increased blood flow would help, but it did nothing.

I slide open the zipper of the suitcase I borrowed from Sophia and fish my hand in. I feel the heel of one of my red shoes. I give it a tug and pull it out.

Reaching down I carefully unbuckle the thick strap around my left ankle. I feel instant relief as I glide my foot out of the sandal.

I slip the red shoe on. It pinches but it's not nearly as uncomfortable as the sandal.

Just as I'm moving to remove the right sandal, the door to the conference room flies open and the woman with the gift bag filled with fragrant smelling handmade soaps darts out.

She doesn't look in my direction, even though we spent the better part of the afternoon talking. Technically, the majority of the time I was listening to her run through her presentation.

I watch in silence as she races through the waiting area before she disappears around the corner and out of sight.

I can't tell if she took off in a rush from the excitement of landing a deal or the devastation of rejection.

I look toward the open conference room door as I tug on the strap around my right ankle.

Dammit. It's so tight that the leather has absolutely no give to it.

"Lenore," a man's voice calls out. "Sweetheart, where are you?"

I'm not surprised by the softness in his tone. I overheard Lenore telling someone earlier that her husband is one of the investors.

I sit silently, tugging on the strap of my sandal.

I have to get it off. If I don't, I'm going to walk into that conference room wearing two different shoes.

I might as well pack up my chances of getting a deal and take them home with me now.

"Lenore?" The man's voice is louder now. I can tell that he's about to walk through the conference room doorway.

He does.

He's older, handsome, and dressed in an expensive three-piece black suit.

"Hi," he offers when his gaze meets mine. "I see that we saved the best for last. You're Mabel's friend, aren't you?"

I nod. "I'm Dexie Walsh."

"You wouldn't happen to know where Lenore is, would you?" He taps the face of the large silver watch on his wrist. "I told her we'd only be here until six. I hope my bride hasn't flown the coop."

I smile at the affection in his eyes when he talks about his wife. "She went to get some water."

I glance down at my watch. It's almost seven. I've been here even longer than I thought.

"I'll go find her." He sets off toward the corridor just as a woman walks out of the conference room.

I know, before she says a word, that she's Mabel's sister. The resemblance is striking.

"You must be Dexie." She tosses me a wave as she follows after Lenore's husband. "I'm Rhoda. Give us two minutes and we'll get started."

Two minutes? I hope to hell that's enough time to rip this sandal off my foot.

I wait until Rhoda is out of view before I grip both hands around the strap of my sandal and pull.

"Dammit," I whisper. "Get off of my foot."

I give it another good, strong yank but it doesn't budge.

I sigh in frustration. "I can't believe this is happening to me."

"I was about to say the same thing." The deep seductive sound of a male voice startles me. "Hello, neighbor."

Chapter 14

Dexie

I stare up at the man who just spoke to me. It's not just any man. *It's him.*

My scorching hot neighbor is standing less than two feet away smiling down at me.

Wow. He's even more gorgeous when two plates of glass aren't separating us.

"Can I help?" He tilts his chin down.

The five-o-clock shadow covering his jaw catches my eye. How can he be just as sexy completely dressed in this waiting room as he is late at night when he has a towel wrapped around his waist?

"I can help with the shoe," he says before I can form a coherent response to his question.

He's on one knee in front of me in an instant.

"I…" my voice trails when his hand brushes against the strap that's biting into my ankle.

"May I?" he asks, his ocean blue eyes locking with mine.

When I was a child, I'd wish for eyes the color of his, instead of the shade of brown that I was born with.

I nod.

Goose bumps pebble my skin the instant his fingertips brush against my ankle. There's no way he doesn't notice the shiver that races through me as he glides his hand over the back of my leg.

"This might pinch," he says smoothly. "You'll feel it tighten for a second before it releases."

I've imagined his voice in my mind but never did it sound this raspy or this warm.

I watch as his long fingers slide the strap loose, the tightening of the leather finally giving way to relief as he slips the sandal from my foot.

"How's that?" He looks back up at me, a smile ghosting his full lips.

"Better," I mutter under my breath, my mouth still bone dry, my pulse racing.

I break his gaze. The intensity is too much. Being this close to him is making my head spin.

"Are you all right?" Concern blankets his tone. "You look flush."

Because you've seen me practically naked.

I bite my tongue to hold those words in place. "I'm fine."

"She needs water." Lenore's voice interrupts us. "She's been sitting in that chair for hours."

He reaches to grab a water bottle that Lenore is pushing at him. He opens it quickly, shoving it into my hand. "Drink. Take a nice long drink."

I grab the plastic bottle. Our fingers touch, sending heat crawling up my skin.

Taking a swallow, I watch as he pushes to his feet. He glances over his shoulder at Lenore, her husband, and Rhoda.

"Let's give her a minute." He motions to the conference room door before he looks back at me. "When you're ready, we'll be waiting for you."

"You'll be waiting for me?" I ask, my voice shaking.

"I'm Rocco Jones." He glances to his right briefly to watch the others enter the conference room. "I'm one of the investors you'll be pitching to."

His outrageously handsome face softens with a smile before he walks away.

What the hell have I gotten myself into?

***

This is going well. At least, I think it's going well.

I look down at my red shoes waiting for another question. Silence fills the space.

Lenore clears her throat. "If there are no more questions for Dexie, we can move onto offers if there are any."

Rhoda's hand is in the air just as Glenn speaks. "Your company name is Dexie Walsh? Have you considered changing it?"

"It's perfect." Rocco's declaration surprises me.

He hasn't said a word since I walked into the conference room and dove into my pitch.

I ran through my sales numbers for the past three years, my marketing approach to date and my vision for my company's future.

Rhoda and Glenn had a long list of questions, but Rocco sat silently studying the handbags I placed on the conference room table in front of them.

He touched two, glanced at my business plan for all of three seconds and then sat back in his chair to watch me while I spoke to Rhoda and Glenn.

The only time he broke a smile was when Lenore asked if I could make her an oversized shoulder bag in red with a gold buckle and trim.

"The name doesn't define the product." Glenn picks up an emerald green clutch to examine the stitching.

"It defines the brand," Rocco counters. "Her name is as unique as she is."

I catch his gaze and smile in gratitude.

I struggled endlessly with a name for my company before I set my business up, but there was nothing that I came up with that captured the essence of my designs as well as my name does.

"I'd like to get a word in," Rhoda jokingly says with a laugh. "I'm ready to make you an offer."

My heart stops for a beat as I absorb those words.

Once Rhoda introduced herself to me, I realized that I'd seen her before. Her picture graced the cover of a financial magazine less than a year ago. She's worth tens of millions of dollars. She's a philanthropist and has helped launch a handful of successful companies, including a shoe brand that is dominating the market today.

She's a perfect fit for me.

She understands what women are looking for in fashion accessories.

"I'm going to need sixty perfect equity in your business, Dexie." She leans both hands on the table in front of her. Her perfectly manicured red nails are striking against the light oak. "You've built a foundation, but it's going to take a lot of money to grow this endeavor of yours to the level I believe it can be."

"Never give up that much equity." Glenn shakes his head.

"Are you making an offer?" Rhoda looks over at him.

Rocco sits stoically in the middle, his gaze trained on my face.

"No." Glenn leans back in his chair. "Lenore will be investing enough of our money into this through all the bags I know she'll be buying."

I smile.

"What about you?" Rhoda reaches to touch Rocco's forearm.

I watch as her fingers play over his skin.

He glances down at her hand. "I agree with Glenn. Sixty perfect equity is too much for Dexie to give up."

I've never heard my name said that way before. His voice is rough, the tone raw.

"That's not an offer, Rocco." Rhoda slides her hand away.

"I'll need time to look over the numbers, but I'm definitely interested," he says, looking up at me.

"If you wait, I may have to rescind my offer." Rhoda casts a gaze in my direction. "Consider that before you walk out of here."

"It's an idle threat." Glenn laughs. "She's horrible at playing hardball."

Rhoda covers her mouth with her hand to hide a wide grin. "I'll have a formal proposal drawn up and sent over to you. Do we have your address, Dexie?"

"I have it." Rubbing his chin, Rocco gives me a devilish smile. "I'll be in touch."

"We will be in touch," Rhoda corrects him with a lift of her brows. "I'm looking forward to working with you, Dexie."

Rocco's jaw flexes. "Don't get ahead of yourself, Rhoda."

"What can you offer her that I can't?" she scoffs.

His gaze shifts from her to me. He tilts his head slightly, raking me from head-to-toe. "I'll see you soon, Ms. Walsh."

I nod.

No one else in the room knows the secret hidden in those seemingly innocent words but the man who spoke them and me.

Chapter 15

Rocco

My gaze follows Dexie as she leaves the room, her ass swaying beneath the demure black dress she's wearing.

The woman is stunning. Petite with lush curves and big, beautiful brown eyes framed with long lashes.

Her pink lips are full; a natural pout graced them when she first looked up and saw me standing in front of her in the waiting room.

I was sure my eyes were playing tricks on me when I walked out of the conference room and spotted her sitting alone.

I didn't need to see her face to know it was the woman who has been captivating me through my window at night.

My cock hardened when she finally turned to me.

I dropped to a knee to not only help her with her shoe but to hide my arousal.

"You're not getting that last one, Rocco." Rhoda taps her fingers on my shoulder. "We both know that I'm the best partner for her."

I turn to face her, taking in the smile that's playing on her red lips. "Bullshit."

That draws a hearty laugh from her. "What do you know about handbags?"

To accentuate her point, she drops her purse on the table. The heavy thud turns Glenn around to look at us both.

"You're not fighting over that last pitch, are you?" He reaches for Lenore's hand. "I was going to suggest the four of us grab dinner, but I'm not going to listen to you two go at each other all night."

"I can't." I pick up my phone and pocket it. "I have plans."

"A hot date?" Rhoda's voice ticks up a notch. "That's one lucky lady."

"I'll be sure to tell my grandmother you said that." I take Rhoda's hand in mine and bring it to my lips to kiss it. "You three have fun."

"We could go in on Dexie's business together," Rhoda proposes with a wink. "Think about how much fun that would be."

I shake my head. "I prefer one-on-one."

"In and out of the boardroom?" she asks with a sly grin.

"That's our cue to leave." Glenn starts toward the conference room door holding tight to his wife's hand. "Everyone out so I can lock up."

***

I raise my hand in a wave as a silver sedan slides into traffic. Glenn, Lenore and Rhoda slipped into it as soon as the driver parked next to the curb.

It's another perk that Glenn has afforded himself.

He has a car and driver to whisk him around Manhattan at the drop of a hat or a push of a button on his phone.

I prefer the subway or an occasional taxi. More often than not, I walk to where I need to be since my office is located in mid-town just a few blocks from my apartment.

The office is an escape and a place to think. It's also where my assistant, Jared, spends most of his time during the day, researching potential business deals for me, and returning calls from people seeking investments that I have zero interest in.

I slide my phone out of my pocket to thumb out a text to Jared. I need him in the office early tomorrow to do some legwork on a few potential partnerships.

He handles the vetting process and if something has promise, he lays out the details for me.

I have every intention of researching Dexie Walsh's burgeoning company on my own.

I look down to pull up Jared's contact info, but the scent of a now-familiar perfume pulls my gaze over my shoulder. It's sweet like summer roses.

I smile when I see who is standing behind me on the sidewalk that stretches along Park Avenue.

Dexie's dark eyes widen when she catches my gaze.

I give her the full attention she deserves by turning around to face her. "Hello again."

Her lips part slightly.

I don't give her a chance to respond. Instead, I step closer. "Are you headed home?"

"I am." Her gaze shifts to the steady stream of traffic behind me. "I've been trying to flag down a taxi, but no luck."

I punch my fingers over the screen of my phone. "An Uber is on its way to pick us up."

"Us?" She blinks at me.

I reach for the handle of her suitcase, brushing my fingers over hers. "We live on the same block, Ms. Walsh. It makes sense to share a ride, no?"

"Yes," she whispers, glancing down at where our hands are still touching. "Please call me Dexie."

Innocence flickers in her expression as her gaze meets mine again. Standing this close to her is different than staring at her across the bridge of distance that separates my apartment from hers.

I see vulnerability in her eyes that I hadn't noticed before.

"Dexie it is," I say as her hand drops from the handle of the suitcase when a dark SUV pulls up to the curb. "This is our ride."

She nods in silence as she steps toward the car. I open the back passenger door for her before I load her suitcase in the back and take the spot in the front next to the driver.

She needs space. I can sense it.

I'll give it to her now, but I have every intention of buying this woman dinner tonight so we can discuss not only our potential business deal but the intense attraction that has been luring us to our windows at night.

Chapter 16

Dexie

I try to exit the SUV with as much poise as I can muster, even though keeping the skirt of my dress below panty level shouldn't matter at this point.

Rocco Jones has seen a lot of my body.

I watch as he retrieves Sophia's heavy suitcase from the back of the vehicle.

We're in front of my building. That should offer me some relief, but it doesn't.

When I go up to my apartment and flick on the light switch, he'll be able to see me through the three large arched windows.

It was a fun and flirtatious game just a few nights ago, but now that we've met, it's different.

The game is over. This is reality.

"Are you free for dinner?" Rocco asks as he sets the suitcase down on the sidewalk next to him. "Do you like French food?"

I haven't caught my breath since I looked up in the waiting room to see him standing there. Spending more time with him tonight feels like too much.

I need time alone, preferably in a place where he can't watch me.

My bathtub.

I can close the bathroom door, turn on soft music and try and process what happened today.

I take a deep breath, sorting my response in my head. I don't want to be rude, but the man has to know that I'm freaking the hell out on the inside, even if I appear somewhat calm on the outside.

"Rocco!"

He turns in the direction of the female voice calling his name. I follow his gaze across the street to where the brunette who was in his apartment the other night is standing, her hand waving in the air. Tonight she's dressed in faded jeans and a white blouse. The black stilettos on her feet transform the outfit from ordinary to sophisticated.

She looks to the left and then the right before she darts out between two parked cars. Her steps are measured and elegant as she closes the distance between her and Rocco.

"Gina," he says when she reaches us. "What are you doing here?"

"You said you might be at the restaurant around six, so I thought I'd meet you there as a surprise." She looks me over, even though her words are meant just for him. "You didn't show up and since there was no answer when I called you, I came to drag you down there."

"I have plans." His hand tightens on the handle of my suitcase.

"Who's your friend?" There's a surprising softness in her tone.

Obviously, she doesn't see me as a threat. Women like her rarely do. She's tall, slim and has the bone structure of a supermodel. This woman is breathtakingly beautiful.

"Dexie Walsh." He smiles when he looks at me. "I'd like you to meet…"

"Gina." Her arms are around me before I can think. "I'm Rocco's cousin."

Cousin?

An unexpected smile blooms deep inside of me.

She steps back from our embrace. "I love your hair. Pink streaks. It all makes sense now."

"What makes sense?" My gaze volleys between her and Rocco.

"Nothing." Rocco rubs his hand over his jaw. "Dexie and I are going to dinner. I'll catch up with you another time, Gina."

The pasted smile on her face doesn't veil the disappointment in her eyes. Her voice comes out soft. "Of course, Rocco. Maybe tomorrow?"

She needs him. I need time to breathe and think.

"I have plans," I say, even though I don't usually consider a bath a plan, but tonight I need it more than I need anything.

Bubbles, candlelight and pizza ordered in will feed my soul and give me a clearer perspective.

"You do?" Rocco's brow arches.

I nod. "I should get going. Thank you for the shared ride back from the meeting."

"The meeting?" Gina's attention turns to her cousin. "What meeting?"

Rocco sighs. "I had a pitch session this afternoon. Dexie is looking for an investor for her handbag company."

"You're going to be business partners?" The shock in Gina's tone dwarfs the surprised expression on her face.

"Maybe," I answer quietly. "I have more than one offer on the table."

Rocco's gaze catches mine. "You'll be accepting mine. I can offer you much more than Rhoda can."

I should have a witty response to toss back at him, but the man is melting me from the inside out with the intenseness of his blue eyes.

"Thank you again." I reach for the handle of the suitcase. "I hope you two enjoy your dinner."

"It was good meeting you." Gina's hand lands on my shoulder. "You're sure you can't join us?"

I shake my head. "I can't."

"I'll be in touch." Rocco's fingers linger on mine as I tighten my grip on the padded metal handle.

"I look forward to talking about my business," I say quietly.

He leans closer, sending my heartbeat racing. "Your business will be just one of the topics we discuss."

The urge to take a step back is strong, but I stay in place.

He's the one who moves, but not before his hand brushes my forearm. "I'll call you tomorrow afternoon if I don't see you before then."

Chapter 17

Rocco

"It's a strange coincidence, isn't it?" Gina looks over to where Marti is standing near the entrance to the restaurant.

"What's a coincidence?"

I haven't been following the conversation since we arrived at Calvetti's. Gina took a call from a friend on our way here, so I was afforded a few minutes of travel time to decompress.

The urge to ask the Uber driver to turn his car around so I could go back to my apartment and sit in the darkness was strong, but I could tell that Gina needed the company.

"You live in the building next to that gorgeous doll, Dexie."

I smile at her description of the captivating woman I can't stop thinking about. "It is a coincidence."

"When we were here last week, you thought you saw her, didn't you?"

I expected the question. I could see the wheels churning in Gina's head as she put the dots together after meeting Dexie earlier.

"Yes," I answer evenly. "We hadn't met at that point."

"But you had noticed her at that point?" The corner of her mouth lifts into a half-smile.

"I thought you wanted to have dinner with me to complain about a guy." I wave to Marti when she glances in our direction. "What's his name and do I need to track him down?"

"You sound just like Nash," she scoffs.

I smile. "You and Nash are on speaking terms again?"

Gina's relationship with both of my younger brothers mirrors the one she has with me. She looks to Nash and Luke for friendship and support, since her only brother is overseas.

"I forgave him for getting involved with my best friend."

The complicated family dynamic that was born from my brother hopping into bed with Gina's roommate impacted everyone.

It might have turned out great if Nash hadn't made promises that he couldn't keep.

He's two years younger than me, but his maturity level is hovering somewhere on par with that of a high school freshman.

"Forget Nash." Gina slices her hand in the air. "Let's talk about Dexie and what's going on between you two."

"Let's not." I lean forward in my chair. "She pitched her business idea. I see potential in it, so I'm going to partner with her."

"It's strictly business?" Skepticism edges her tone. "Or is there some pleasure too?"

Defining what's been going on between Dexie and I would be near impossible, so I don't put in the effort to do so. "It's business."

"There's more to life than business," Marti says as she approaches our table. "If your grandfather were alive he'd tell you to work just enough to have time left for fun."

Gina playfully rolls her eyes. "My work is fun."

Marti shrugs. "I'll never understand how you survive by taking pictures with your phone, Gina."

It's the simplest terms, but it essentially defines my cousin's livelihood.

Gina earned a degree in behavioral science. Her long-term career path may not have been clear at the time, but no one in the family anticipated that she'd earn a living posting content about fashion and fitness on social media.

She monetizes her accounts and so far, it's paying her bills.

"We weren't talking about me." Gina reaches for Marti's hand. "We were talking about Rocco's new business partner."

"Another new one?" Marti's brows pop. "How many partners do you need before you have enough money?"

"This one is extra special," Gina interjects before I can answer the question.

"How so?" Marti's attention is squared on me.

"She has a brilliant mind for design," I say.

"And a beautiful face," Gina adds.

Marti's face lights up. "You'll bring this new partner in for lunch one day, Rocco."

It's not a question, but a demand.

"We'll see." My mouth curves. "I need to make the deal first."

"It's always dollars first." She pats my shoulder. "I'll check on your linguine."

"We ordered the minestrone," Gina whispers as Marti starts toward the kitchen.

"She made the linguine herself." I laugh. "We'll eat it."

***

Darkness is all that greets me when I enter my apartment an hour later.

I don't switch on any of the lights in the main living space. There's no reason to.

Dexie's not there to see me.

I stand next to the window and gaze into her place. The sky is overcast tonight, so the moon is shrouded behind clouds.

The only light that dots the near horizon is from the apartment above Dexie's.

I have no idea who lives there. I don't pay attention. I've never bothered to glance into their lives and what happens behind the sheer curtains that are meant to separate their movements from the curiosity seekers who live in my building.

I don't care about any of them.

It's Dexie that I long to see. I want to see her.

I look down at my phone, scrolling through my contact list until I land on her name.

I saved the phone number that was included on the pitch sheet Lenore handed to me before Dexie walked into the conference room.

I can text her or call her.

I can interrupt her evening to tell her that I want to talk business, but it's a lie.

I want to talk about the way she dances near her kitchen sink when she thinks no one's watching her or the softness of her movements when she slides out of bed each morning.

I pocket my phone and curse under my breath.

Tonight I won't be catching a glimpse of the beauty across the street. Restlessness eats at me. I won't be able to sleep, so I head to my bedroom to change my clothes.

I'll hit the gym to work off the tension I feel. Hopefully, by the time I come home, Dexie will be in her bed. Alone.

Chapter 18

Dexie

I see Rocco as soon as I round the corner.

He's standing in front of the bodega that occupies the ground floor of his building. His attention is glued to the phone in his hand. He must respond to hundreds of texts and take dozens of calls a day from the people he's partnered with.

The man has invested in several successful start-ups the past few years. He also knows how to play poker like a champ. That makes perfect sense since he held the title of world champion two years in a row.

My sudden wealth of knowledge about Rocco Jones is directly related to the fact that I spent last night at Sophia's apartment. My air conditioner ground to a halt right after I got out of the bathtub.

I thought I could handle the heat, but that lasted all of an hour before I took Sophia up on her offer to bunk at her place.

Once she was tucked into her bed with her handsome husband, I searched out Rocco's name on the browser on my phone.

I barely slept a wink.

I don't see how I can get past Rocco without him noticing me, so I take a proactive approach and clear my throat. "Good morning."

He turns at the sound of my voice and rakes me from head-to-toe.

We may both be dressed in white T-shirts and jeans, but he'd win the *who wore it better* battle between the two of us.

His shoulders are broad and his biceps are impressive.

I look down at the sidewalk to stop myself from staring.

"Dexie," he growls my name out as he closes the short distance between us.

How can his voice send a jolt of desire through me?

"I tried calling you." He waves his phone in the air. "It went straight to voicemail."

That's because I used up all its battery in my mission to learn everything I possibly could about him.

"The battery died." I scratch the back of my head. "I didn't want to wake my friend to ask for a charger."

"Friend?" He cocks a dark brow. "You stayed over at a friend's place last night?"

Considering the fact that it's not even eight a.m. and I have a serious case of bedhead, he shouldn't be surprised.

"My air conditioning wasn't working," I offer.

I don't owe him any explanations. Besides, he must have noticed that I wasn't in my apartment last night when he got home from having dinner with his cousin.

His gaze skims the front of my shirt, lingering on my breasts.

Shit. I'm not wearing a bra.

In my rush to get home, I stuffed my bra into my bag and raced out of Sophia's apartment. My T-shirt isn't see-through, but my nipples are hard at the moment, courtesy of Rocco's muscular body and those blue eyes.

"It's going to be another hot one today." I follow those words with an awkward laugh and a fan of my hand in front of my face. "I need to get up to my place to get ready for work."

"You work in marketing at Matiz Cosmetics."

It's a statement, not a question. Since I didn't include that information on my pitch sheet, he's also gone on a fishing trip online to find out more about me.

That shouldn't excite me as much as it is. He's considering investing in my company. It's understandable that he would research my background.

I nod. "My boss likes me to be there by nine a.m., and since I took the day off yesterday, I can't be late."

I start to brush past him, but his words stop me. "Resign, Dexie. You should stop working at Matiz."

***

"Resign?" I drop my hands to my hips.

I've been waiting to throw that word back at him for the past five minutes.

His phone started ringing as soon as he said that I should quit my job at Matiz.

I waited while he talked about setting up a meeting with someone named Silas to sign a contract.

He kept his eyes on mine during the call. I didn't want to jump to any conclusions, so I took a few breaths to calm down.

We met yesterday. Why does he think he has a right to tell me to quit the job I love, or... at least like? I don't mind going to Matiz five days a week.

"Yes," he answers succinctly, as though that's going to be enough for me.

"Why would I quit my job?" I ask as my gaze drops to my watch.

A shower is out of the question at this point. I'm going to have to run a brush through my hair, do a quick change of clothes, splash on some Matiz perfume and apply my makeup on the subway if I want to be at my desk by nine.

Thankfully, I usually only wear a light dusting of foundation powder, mascara and pale pink gloss on my lips. They're all Matiz products.

He smiles. Those impossibly gorgeous lips of his part and his tongue slips out to moisten his bottom lip.

If that's meant to distract me, it's working.

This man is delicious.

"When we partner, I'll need your attention twenty-four, seven." He steps closer to me, lowering his voice. "I won't tolerate any outside distractions since I'll be investing so much into you."

I stare at his mouth before my gaze slides to his eyes.

"If you want to be successful, you'll need to put everything into our business," he goes on, "I expect great things from you."

"Great things," I repeat back with a bob of my head.

I feel like I'm under a spell. If it's like this now, how will I keep my composure if we become business partners?

I shake off the daze I'm in. "I need to get to work."

"You'll think about what I said?"

I draw in a deep breath. "I need to consider my other options. You're not the only one interested."

"In you?" His dark brows draw together.

I answer the question with a smile, then turn and march into my building.

Chapter 19

Rocco

My morning was easy. I sat at my desk and ran through the notes that I'd saved to my phone yesterday during the pitch meeting.

Offering a deal on the spot isn't a rarity for me. I know a diamond in the rough when I see it.

Yesterday's session had more potential than most, but I only walked away with a solid promise for one partnership. That's with the owner of the pet-grooming product. My instinct didn't steer me wrong on that one. I know because Jared was practically jumping up and down when I ran it past him earlier.

If I rely on his good word, every dog owner in the city is going to be lining up when it launches.

Right now, I have my assistant studying the business models from a handful of the people who have contacted me directly this month either through email or a phone call.

If he sees merit in any of them, he'll put together a spreadsheet, including the sales numbers to date and margins for the product or products. I'll make a decision about whether or not to meet with the business owners based on that information.

My attention is on something more important than any of that.

I have the financials for Dexie Walsh's company in front of me. I'm not blown away by what I'm looking at.

She's a one-woman operation. She handles all aspects of her business entirely on her own while balancing a full-time job.

Scaling her business up would require a substantial monetary investment on my part, as well as a hell of a lot of handholding.

I'm all for the handholding. I've wanted to touch the beauty since I first got a glimpse of her through the window of my apartment.

Investing in her dream is an entirely different thing.

"What's that?" Jared asks as he strolls into my office looking like he belongs on a yacht in the Hamptons.

The peach colored polo shirt and long shorts he has on is typical Jared.

His self-appointed mission to transform me into a slightly older version of him didn't make it out of the starting gate.

He pushes his brown hair back from his forehead. "Are you holding out on me, boss? That's another pitch you're considering, isn't it?"

"Handbags." I lean back in my desk chair. "It's a tough space to make a mark."

"Near impossible." He pulls the wooden chair in the corner closer to my desk before he turns it around and sits, resting his forearms on the back. "It's cutthroat. It would take a huge chunk of change to get any leverage at all."

His words confirm my thoughts. I knew as soon as Dexie started her pitch yesterday that she was facing an uphill battle.

The market is crowded. Trying to get a foot in the door won't be easy.

"What do the numbers look like?" He cranes his head to get a better look at the paper in front of me.

I pick it up and hand it to him. There are no secrets between Jared and me. I trust him to tell me what he honestly thinks.

His word is never the last, but I weigh his opinion with my own and make a decision based on all the data.

He glances at the paper. "Dexie Walsh is the company's name?"

"And the owner's name," I confirm with a nod.

"Cute." He smiles. "It's unique, catchy. I like it."

I like the woman it belongs to, but Jared doesn't need to know that. I've never introduced a woman I'm interested in personally to him. I don't foresee that changing.

"Is this in your *maybe* pile?" He drops the document on my desk.

"For now." That's the easy answer I give him. I have every intention of working out a deal with Dexie that will benefit both of us.

He stands and drags the chair back to its spot near my office door. "I have one to add to that and three I suggest we pass on."

"Call the passes and wish them well." I push to my feet. "We'll go over the other one tomorrow."

"You're taking off?" There's no surprise in his tone. Jared's well aware that I'm not the nine-to-five type.

I round the desk and yank a gray suit coat from a hook on the rack near the doorway. "There's someone I need to see."

***

"Is Ms. Walsh expecting you?" The woman behind the reception desk at Matiz Cosmetics gives me the once-over.

"Yes," I lie with a smile.

"You said your name is Mr. Jones?" She blinks. "Is this a business matter?"

"It's Rocco Jones. Ms. Walsh will know what it's concerning."

She hesitates, glancing at the computer screen in front of her. "I'll call her line and see if she's available."

She does just that, poking a few buttons on the phone on her desk before she speaks into the receiver. "There's a Mr. Rocky Jones here to see you, Ms. Walsh."

"Rocco," I correct her with a grin.

She ignores that with a scowl.

I glance down the long corridor, but the only movement is the leaf of a large potted plant being blown by the overhead air conditioning.

"I'll tell him," she says and then hangs up the phone. Her attention shifts from it to me. "Ms. Walsh will be able to see you in ten minutes. If you'd like to wait, you can do so in the visitors' lounge."

I look to the left, and then the right. "Where might that be?"

She gestures behind me to a row of fabric-covered chairs that border the wall opposite her desk. "There."

She can call it whatever she likes. I take a seat in what is obviously a generic waiting area. The walls are painted a neutral tan. The carpeting on the floor is the same hue.

From what I've seen so far, the marketing department of Matiz Cosmetics is boring as hell. It's nothing like the woman I'm here to see.

I'm curious to find out how the hell she ended up working here.

Chapter 20

Dexie

My office doesn't have the same view out the window as my apartment. Most people would consider the views from the Matiz Cosmetics Tower spectacular. I'm not one of them. I much prefer to glance through a plate of glass to see Rocco Jones in all his half-naked glory.

The vision of Central Park and the tops of the sun-touched buildings beyond that I'm witness to each day is breathtaking in its own right, but it's not what I wish I were staring at right now.

What I want to be looking at is Rocco Jones handsome face, and apparently, that's waiting for me in the visitors' lounge.

I stare at the late afternoon blue sky, debating whether to invite Rocco into my office or to the café across the street.

Coffee is ridiculously expensive there because of the Fifth Avenue address, but that hasn't deterred anyone who works in this building or the others that line this block.

If the man wants to discuss my purse business, I'd prefer if that happened outside the confines of the Matiz offices.

My co-workers all know that my dream is to own a brand that rivals that of the boutique on the corner. You can walk out of there with a handbag that costs as much as six months worth of my rent.

I want the notoriety without the high price tag.

The jarring sound of my cell phone ringing breaks through my thoughts. I fumble in my purse for it, yanking it out and swiping my finger over the screen before I bother to look down to see who is calling.

Sophia calls me almost every afternoon when she hits the four o'clock lull.

She needs that extra push to get her through to the end of the day. It's either a candy bar or gossiping with me that helps her climb the hill to quitting time.

"So you didn't give in to temptation today?" I joke before she can say anything.

"Actually…" a man's voice on the other end of the call startles me. "I did give in to temptation. That's the reason why I'm still sitting in the visitors' lounge waiting to see you."

"Rocco?" I ask although I know it's him. My body has never reacted this way to another man's voice. *Ever.*

My nipples have stiffened into tight points under my pink dress; my core aches.

I slump into the chair behind my desk and close my eyes.

The café it is.

At least there, I can tame my desire and focus on business.

"I've been waiting for close to an hour, Dexie." He sighs, the sound more of a rumble than a breathless release. "I'll wait forever, but I'd prefer not to."

I took an important call after Shona let me know he was here. I lost track of time. Daydreaming about his ripped abs after the call didn't help.

"I'll be right out," I say softly. "Wait right there."

There's a low chuckle before he says anything. "I won't move a muscle."

Muscle.

My thoughts float back to this morning and how he looked in that tight white T-shirt.

"See you soon," I say in a too-high voice.

"Soon," he repeats back in a dangerously low tone.

"Shit," I mutter under my breath after I end the call. "Get it together, Dexie."

All the encouraging self-talk in the world isn't going to help me. I have to go and face the man who may be instrumental in making all of my professional dreams come true, even though he's the star of every one of my personal fantasies.

***

I feel like I'm strutting a runway as I saunter down the narrow corridor that leads to the reception area.

My office is to the right where the junior executives and up-and-comers all work. The wider corridor that leads to the left is where the senior marketing staff's offices are.

My promotion six months ago landed me a small office and the title of Marketing Specialist. Essentially, I'm straddling the line between newbie and junior manager.

I watch Rocco as I take measured steps toward where he's sitting.

His gaze is once again cast down to his phone, his fingers blazing a trail over the screen.

I'm grateful that his attention is occupied.

My nipples have yet to calm the hell down and the thin fabric of my wrap dress leaves little to the imagination.

I'm less than three feet from him when his head pops up and his eyes take me in. He rakes me slowly from head-to-toe, his lips parting just ever so slightly.

He's on his feet by the time I'm standing in front of him.

Nothing about him has changed since this morning other than the suit jacket that now covers his T-shirt and the start of a shadow of whiskers over his jaw.

"Do you feel like getting a coffee?" I look up at his face as I ask the question, my voice as controlled as I can manage.

He stares at me for a minute. "There's a place across the street that sells a great cup. We can go there."

I nod as I turn to Shona. She's doing her best to look busy behind the reception desk. "If Mr. Dirks calls, can you forward it to my cell, Shona?"

She tosses me a smile. "Will do."

I take in a breath and point toward the bank of elevators. "I'm all yours."

That lures a devilish grin to Rocco's mouth. "Lucky, lucky me."

Chapter 21

Rocco

Pink perfection.

That's what Dexie Walsh is.

The dress she's wearing was made for her body. It hugs her in all the right places, including her beautiful breasts.

The neckline dips enough that I got a clear view of the top of her round tits as we took the short walk from her office building to this café.

My café.

I hold a sixty-six percent interest in this place.

My cousin, Arlo Calvetti and his wife, Palla, own the other thirty-three percent. They're the ones who are here at the crack of dawn each day, readying to serve the caffeinated needs of the people rushing to the businesses that border this street.

Arlo approached me when his job as a senior buyer for a pharmaceutical company was cut four years ago. This storefront was home to a small investment firm at the time. They relocated to an office in one of the towers on Park Avenue.

The dream for Arlo was a high-end café that only serves the finest blends of beans from around the world. I hopped on board with the understanding that this is a hands-off endeavor for me.

I hold the bulk of the purse strings until they can buy me out.

Palla on Fifth will be his family's legacy.

"It's my treat," Dexie announces as we near the barista counter. Her hand disappears into the large purple bag slung over her shoulder.

Her hair moves with each dive of her hand. It's loose and in waves. I watch her intently, noticing the small diamond piercing in her nose.

I hadn't seen that before. I'm not surprised. I could stare at her for hours on end, and discover something new with each blink of my eyes.

The freckle that sits above her left brow was the focus of some of my attention this morning. Admittedly, her nipples stole the show.

"I'll get the coffee." I take a step closer to the counter.

She pushes to get in front of me. "How do you take your coffee?"

I smile inwardly at her determination to pay. She's independent. I like that. It's refreshing in my world.

I'm a generous man. I've used my wealth to help those around me. It's unusual for someone else to pull out his or her wallet to pay for anything for me.

"Hot," I answer succinctly. "No cream or sugar."

She blinks up at me. "Hot?"

"Extra, extra hot." I glance at her full lips.

"I'll order it that way." She turns to face the barista counter, shielding the blush on her face from my view.

I stand aside as she orders and pays, noting that she likes two sugars and a splash of cream in her coffee.

"The barista said someone will bring it to our table." That pulls a small laugh from her. "I told them I could wait for it at the counter, but he insisted we sit."

I motion toward an unoccupied table near the entrance. "How's that?"

Her gaze circles the café. It's packed, as usual. I've never dropped in to find it vacant, which I'm grateful for.

"Sure." She nods, brushing past me to make her way to one of the two wooden chairs next to the circular table.

I wait until she sits before I lower myself onto the chair next to her with my back to the counter.

She wrings her hands together in front of her. "I wasn't expecting to see you this afternoon."

Of course she wasn't. After our brief encounter on the sidewalk outside her building this morning, she put all of her focus on work.

"Have you heard from Rhoda?"

She runs her fingertips over her temple, her eyes closing briefly. "No, not yet."

I anticipated as much. Rhoda will take her time to gather an arsenal of hard numbers and facts to show Dexie. She'll argue her case for a large chunk of equity and use the persuasive power of future profits to lure Dexie to sign something she'll quickly regret.

Rhoda has a good heart, but when it comes to a deal like this, she has a shrewd business sense.

"I'm a better partner for you," I say, rubbing my hand over my jaw.

I don't mince words because there's no need to. I am the better partner. I'll treat her fairly and I'll make her work hard for the inevitable success she'll achieve.

"I would be remiss if I didn't hear Rhoda out." She smiles past me, her gaze darting over my shoulder. "There's Palla. She runs this place."

I met Palla a decade ago when she walked into my grandmother's restaurant on the arm of Arlo.

I was having dinner with his father, my uncle, Robbie.

I witnessed my uncle meeting the woman of his son's dreams. Marti called it that night, telling Palla that she would be the newest member of the Calvetti clan within a year.

They married eight months later.

Palla is next to us with a cup of coffee in each hand before a word leaves my mouth.

"I knew it was you, Rocco." She puts one cup in front of me. "You're the only person I know who orders their coffee extra, extra hot."

I move to stand, taking her in for a quick embrace. "How are you?"

"Happy." She pats her round belly. "Three more months."

"How do the other five feel about this one?" I dip my chin. "Have you told them?"

Her gaze drops to Dexie before it settles back on my face. "I had to. Joey asked if I ate too many pancakes, so I had to tell them."

Joey is the oldest of her and Arlo's brood. They've been blessed with two sets of twins, all boys and a golden-haired two-year-old princess named after Marti.

"You look stunning today, Dex." She reaches for Dexie's hand. "So you two know each other?"

"Palla!" A woman's voice rises above the noise in the café. "Shipment's here."

"I have to go." She gives Dexie's hand another squeeze before she pats my shoulder. "A woman's work is never done."

I watch her walk away and then take my seat.

"The last time I was in here, Palla was pregnant with her daughter." Dexie sips her coffee. "I can't believe she remembered my name."

"I can." I lock eyes with her. "You're unforgettable."

Chapter 22

Dexie

His words are inching us closer to a discussion about our window game of chance.

There might have been a chance that I would catch a glimpse of his cock one night, but that ship has sailed. Game over.

There's no way that we can work together to build my business by day only to flash each other at the window by night.

They don't go hand-in-hand.

"We were talking about Rhoda before Palla came over." I divert with a sugary sweet smile.

He takes another sip of his still very hot coffee, his eyes glued to mine. "You're not going to partner with Rhoda."

"I'll decide after I hear what you both have to offer."

The ghost of a grin that touches his mouth tells me he likes that answer. His words say otherwise. "Rhoda doesn't have the same vision for your company that I do."

I sigh. "I don't know what her vision is so I can't rule it out."

He rakes a hand through his already messy hair. It just makes him hotter and I think he knows it.

Men like him parade around the city leaving a string of broken hearts in their wake. He's almost too good-looking if such a thing exists.

My phone buzzes in my purse. I fish it out and look at the number on the screen. It's Sophia.

"Is that Mr. Dirks?" Rocco leans back in his chair. "Are you still on the clock?"

I nod, realizing that he was paying very close attention to what I said to Shona before we left my office. "I should get back to work."

I don't correct his assumption that the call is work-related. I do need to finish a few things before I can call it a day at Matiz, including touching base with Rio Dirks, the stylist I hired for an upcoming fragrance photo shoot.

"Let's meet for dinner later." He moves to stand. "We'll talk about what I'm prepared to offer you."

I'll give him an A-plus for persistence. Rhoda is hovering right around a D at the moment since I haven't heard a word from her.

"Say around seven," he goes on. "I know a great French place. That's if you're free, of course."

I can't exactly lie and say I have plans. He can see straight into my apartment. He's bound to notice me sitting on my sofa eating popcorn and watching a movie.

My gaze drops to my phone again when it chimes. This time it's a text message from my best friend.

Sophia: *Nicholas is in Boston tonight so come over so we can cheese fondue. You know how much he hates it.*

I read it twice. This has to be fate.

I look up at Rocco. If we plan on talking business, I prefer not to be gazing at him over candlelight while I'm holding a glass of robust red wine in my hand.

I counter his offer with one of my own. It's not ideal, but it works for me. "What about lunch tomorrow?"

His response is immediate. "I'll have something brought into my office. I'll text you the address. You text me the time."

His office?

I stand too, feeling like he somehow won our battle of wits, even though it feels like I was the only one playing.

"Tomorrow it is." I take a step back from the table. "I'll see you then."

"If not before," he says with a lift of his brow.

The innuendo in his words isn't hidden at all.

Unless fondue takes all night, Rocco is going to be standing at his window when I get home.

***

It turns out cheese fondue takes a lot longer than I expected.

A lot of that had to do with the fact that Sophia was getting the fondue ready while I read bedtime stories to her daughter, Winter.

I couldn't stop at just one, so story time seeped into the nine o'clock hour and now I'm standing in my apartment after midnight wishing I hadn't indulged in that much rich food so late.

My place is dark. I skipped past the overhead light switch and headed straight to the window as soon as my door was locked.

There's a light on in Rocco's apartment, but he's not in sight.

Disappointment rushes over me, even though I kept telling myself on the subway ride home, that I didn't want him to undress for me tonight.

Of course, I did. I do.

Who wouldn't? The man has the body of a Greek God and a face that can stop traffic.

Glancing down at my watch, I blow out a heavy sigh.

I need to rest. I have a morning filled with meetings tomorrow, followed by lunch with my neighbor.

I steal one more look at his window before I slip out of my dress and into my bed.

The soulful sound of music coming from the apartment across the hall, lulls me to sleep with thoughts of Rocco on my mind.

Chapter 23

Rocco

I gaze down at my desk and the take-out containers.

Chinese food.

I know Dexie likes it. I watched her eat it after it was delivered to her apartment one night.

Jesus. If she knew that, she'd order Harold to install blinds on the windows of her apartment today.

"Do you need anything else?" Jared's voice pulls me from my thoughts.

"Privacy."

"I figured as much." He adjusts the tips of the navy bow tie around his neck.

I give him the once-over. His dark blue pants are tailored. The pinstriped shirt he's wearing isn't off the rack.

He's dressed to the nines today, so I ask the obvious question. "Do you have a job interview?"

"Where the hell would I find a job that pays me as much as you do?" He huffs out a laugh. "I'm here until you die, Rocco."

"I get the message." I nod. "I would have preferred a different delivery."

"Fine," he spits out. "I'm here until you retire, so don't do that for at least another thirty years. I need to pay off the mortgage on my apartment."

I smile. "Duly noted."

He glances over his shoulder at his desk. "I'm having lunch with someone."

"A date?" I cross my arms over my chest. "Do I know her?"

"You haven't met," he says, scratching the base of his neck. "She's related to a client."

That should sound an alarm for me, but it doesn't. Silas tuned me into what was going on when he texted me a picture two nights ago of Jared at a bar with him and his sister.

My assistant couldn't take his eyes off of the woman.

My silence is enough to spur Jared to confess. "Fine. I'm crushing hard for Silas's sister, Monique, all right?"

"Crushing hard?" I cock a brow. "How old are you again?"

"Old enough to know that I sound like an idiot when I talk like that." He laughs. "I'm taking off and I can't promise I'll be back today."

I'd balk at that, but I'm hoping that Dexie is going to extend her lunch hour beyond sixty minutes. "I'll see you tomorrow, Jared. Enjoy."

He's out of the office before I can get another word in.

It's fucking perfect.

I'm getting everything I want.

Time alone with Dexie Walsh and the chance to talk about all those nights spent at our windows.

I missed her last night because I hit the gym at midnight to work off my restless energy, but if our meeting goes well, tonight will be different.

Glass won't be separating us; nothing will be.

***

"I want to be transparent." She bites on the corner of her bottom lip. "I mean, I need to be transparent."

I need to be fucking you.

I shake those words away, instead shifting my focus from her mouth to her eyes.

Her left iris is slightly darker than the right.

I've never met a woman as unique as Dexie Walsh.

"I'm meeting Rhoda tomorrow to talk about my business. We're having a drink after work."

Her chest heaves on a sigh and my eyes drop to the front of the cream-colored dress she's wearing.

It fits her like a glove.

I noticed the dress the second she walked in and when she brushed past me to toss her purse onto Jared's desk, her ass grabbed my full attention.

The fabric is hugging her every curve.

"You're wasting your time, Dexie." I close the empty take-out container in front of me.

The food wasn't half-bad. I may indulge again, but only if she's by my side.

"I knew you'd say that," she mutters.

I smile at the slight dig. I like her spirit and the fact that she's not falling all over herself trying to secure a deal with me.

"I'll have my proposal in your hands soon." I take a sip of water before I place the bottle back down on my desk.

I took the wooden chair in front of my desk and offered Dexie the office chair behind it. It's moderately more comfortable.

Her gaze scans the room. "I didn't picture your office looking like this."

I've never seen the value in paying a premium to rent office space I'll rarely be in.

This two-room space is big enough to house Jared's desk in the waiting area and mine in the main office.

It's uncommon for any of my business associates to stop by here. I can count on one hand how many face-to-face meetings I've taken white sitting behind this desk.

"I didn't picture you working in an office like Matiz." I sit back in my chair. "Tell me how you ended up working there."

She takes a breath. "The staffing agency I went to hooked me up with Matiz."

It's a succinct answer. She plays her cards close to the vest. My time at the poker table has taught me how to read people, including beautiful women.

"Is the job more important than Dexie Walsh?"

"My company?" she clarifies with a raised brow.

I study her face. "Or the woman. You decide."

She considers her answer. "It's not more important, but it's essential."

Most of the entrepreneurs I've worked with have handed me the same song and dance at the beginning of our partnerships. I get it. I've always understood.

Everyone needs money for the essentials. You can't pay rent, buy food or clothe yourself without cash. Hope is not currency in the real world.

It is in mine.

I pay my partners to immerse themselves in their dream.

My offers always include a salary if the person I'm working with hasn't taken the leap to full-time goal chaser.

Dexie isn't there yet. I understand, but I want to hear it from her.

"I have a degree in marketing," she goes on without any prompting from me. "I moved to New York so I could see first-hand how the big names are selling their handbags. I study all the online ads that the designer brands run. I pick them apart until I understand every nuance. The font of the text is vital. The color of the background can make or break a sale."

I don't interrupt. Instead, I lean forward and focus on every word she's saying.

"I took the position at Matiz because their marketing department is brilliant. I could get by with working part-time for my friend, Sophia. She heads a clothing line. I learn something every time I work a fashion show with her, but I crave the knowledge I get from my job." Her hands knit together on the desk. "When it comes to marketing a product, whether it's a tube of mascara or a tote bag, every aspect matters and if I don't understand each small thing, I'm not putting the value on my brand that it deserves."

I almost rise to my feet to give her a standing ovation.

"Impressive," I say quietly. "Your approach is impressive."

"I have to choose the partner who will complement my approach. I know that you understand."

"You think Rhoda is that person?"

She draws her bottom lip between her teeth, her eyes searching my face. "I think a partnership with Rhoda would be less…"

"Complicated?"

Her cheeks bloom pink. "I don't live next door to Rhoda."

I lower my voice even though we're the only two people here. "You mean Rhoda hasn't seen you almost naked."

Working on a quick swallow, she bats her long eyelashes. "I was stunned when I saw you at the pitch session."

"The feeling was mutual." I inch forward on my chair. "Imagine my surprise when I walked out of the conference room and found you sitting there. It took my breath away."

Chapter 24

Dexie

Rocco knows the impact of his words.

I see it on his face. His mouth curved up when I swallowed hard after he told me that seeing me in the waiting room at the pitch session took his breath away.

Breaking our gaze, I glance down at his desk and the take-out containers and chopsticks.

I ordered food from the same place the first night I moved into my new apartment.

I was surprised to see he'd ordered it for lunch, although the restaurant is only a few blocks from here.

I was more taken aback by the way he's dressed. He's wearing a light blue button-down shirt that's open at the collar and a pair of black pants.

Part of me wonders if he traded in the T-shirts and jeans to impress me.

"Dexie," he says my name gently, luring my head up. "Let's talk about this. Let's talk about what's going on between us."

I study his face. It was so much easier when he was a nameless stranger that I watched through my window at night. Now, he's my potential business partner.

"What's there to talk about?" I try to sound flippant, but I know the expression on my face gives me away.

I'm confused.

I've never been this attracted to a man before. If I hadn't run into him at the pitch meeting, I would still be racing home each night to stand at my window to stare at him.

"You liked what you saw when you looked into my apartment."

It's a declaration that I can't deny. I was practically drooling all over the pane of glass when he had the towel wrapped around his waist.

"I liked what I saw," he goes on, his gaze drifting over my face. "I want to see more."

So do I but I want a business partner more. At least, I think I do.

I lean back in the chair. "Things are different now, Rocco."

"Why?"

I rub my hand over my forehead. "There's a chance that we're going to be working together. My company is my life. I feel like I'm on the cusp of finally getting what I want and I can't risk that."

His eyes narrow. "You don't think we can get to know each other on a personal level at the same time we enter a business partnership?"

"I don't have any experience in that," I say honestly. "Do you?"

The way his jaw tightens answers my question for me. He's fucked other women that he's partnered with.

It makes sense. He's a handsome man with a body that makes me weak in the knees. His other female business partners must feel the same attraction to him that I do.

Rhoda just rose on my sliding scale from a D to an A-plus.

I won't be stung with a needle of jealousy whenever I hear her talk about who else she is partnering with.

I'm not naïve enough to think that sex with Rocco would lead to a relationship, but intimacy without at least some familiarity attached to it doesn't work for me.

I'm not looking for a promise of exclusivity before I go down on a man, but I like to know something about him beyond what excites him in bed.

My phone buzzes. I reach down and fish in my purse for it. I scan the screen before I silence it.

Rising to my feet, I scrub my hand over my forehead. "I need to get back to work."

He's out of his chair. "I'll go with you. We'll continue our discussion on the way."

I shoulder my bag and round his desk. "You don't need to do that."

He steps in front of me. It's not a move meant to intimidate me. I can see that in the tenderness in his eyes. He's concerned or maybe curious. There's something unspoken lingering in his expression.

"I can't ignore what's happening between us." His voice is deep. "I'm very attracted to you. I want to get to know you better."

I want the same thing, but it's not as cut and dry as he seems to think it is.

"I have an important decision to make about who I want to partner with." I sigh. "This is a big deal to me and I don't want to fuck it up by letting my attraction to you cloud my judgment."

His mouth curves into a smile. "You admit that you're attracted to me?"

I hold his gaze, my lips parting. "I need to get back to work."

His hand jumps to my face, his thumb grazing a path over the corner of my mouth.

For the briefest moment I think he's going to kiss me, and I know that I won't stop him, but that's not what happens.

He brings his thumb to his mouth and flicks his tongue over the pad of it. "Lemon sauce and you. Delicious."

Arousal perks deep inside me.

I take a deep breath and move back one full step. "Thank you for lunch."

"It was my pleasure. I'll be in touch."

"See you soon," I say before I realize the weight of those words.

"Indeed," he shoots back as I walk past him on my way out the door.

Chapter 25

Dexie

"If I weren't a very happily married woman, I'd be baking some muffins to take over to your neighbor's apartment right about now."

I bark out a laugh. "What?"

Sophia glances back at me from her perch on my windowsill. "I spot at least four hot men over there. Is your neighbor one of them?"

He's the hottest. Just look for the messy brown hair, the chiseled jaw and the lips that look like they'd take you to heaven and back.

I can't say those words to Sophia because she'd set to work baking something, anything that I could take over to Rocco.

"Aren't you the one who is always telling your daughter that it's rude to stare?" I dump a pouch of microwave popcorn into a large ceramic bowl. "You've been sitting there since you got here, Sophia."

"There is nothing on television that will compare to this." She motions for me to hand the bowl to her. "Come sit next to me."

I shake my head. "Try and pull yourself away from that and join me on the couch."

Her gaze flits back to Rocco's apartment. "It looks like they're going to play cards."

It makes sense. Rocco isn't a stranger to a deck of cards. The million dollar purses he collected when he was playing professional poker are proof of that.

"We can play cards," I offer with a laugh. "What's that card game that you're always playing with Nicholas?"

"Strip poker."

I turn to look at her. "You don't know the first thing about poker."

"That's why it's my husband's favorite game." She slips the strap of her red tank top down her shoulder. "I'm always nude before he sheds one piece of clothing. He likes it that way."

I laugh. "You two are relationship goals. You know that, right?"

She stretches her legs, readying to stand. "I know that if I were you, I'd be borrowing a cup of sugar from that man in the next building."

"You don't even know which one is my neighbor." Reaching for the remote, I settle on the couch.

"My money is on the one in the blue shirt." She stands, yanking up the waistband of her black yoga pants. "I caught him looking over here. I can't say he's as hot as Nicholas, but he's close, Dex."

I scroll through the channels, oblivious to what is on any of them.

I haven't stopped thinking about Rocco since I left his office this afternoon.

When I first got home from work an hour ago, he already had company. I ducked into my bathroom, took a shower and put on a pair of white shorts and a blue T-shirt.

I tried to avoid looking at his apartment, but my willpower was no match for my curiosity.

When I did finally glance in that direction, I was met with his gaze and then a lift of his hand in a wave.

That's when Sophia called to ask if she could drop by to show me a few new sketches for her spring collection.

I welcomed the distraction until she walked in and headed straight to the window.

"Bring your sketchpad here," I say, patting the couch next to me. "Show me what you're working on."

"In a minute." Her hands fall to her hips. "Why are you doing everything you can to avoid looking over at your neighbor? Is there something you need to tell me about the two of you?"

I've thought about telling her that Rocco is one of the investors who are interested in partnering with me, but I don't want to tell Sophia any half-truths. I'm not ready to confess that I treated him to a slow striptease through the window.

"I'm doing everything I can to have some time with my best friend." I shoot her a smile. "I'm eager to see the sketches so show me."

Her eyes brighten. "I think you're going to love them, Dex. I'll use the ladies' room while you get us some water."

I get up from the couch and head to the kitchen.

I can't keep my eyes from sneaking a peek at Rocco's apartment.

He's on his feet. His hands are shoved into the pockets of the pants he was wearing earlier at his office. His dress shirt is still as freshly pressed as it was then.

He's standing by the window, but he's not looking at me.

His gaze is cast to the sky.

The men seated behind him are laughing. Poker chips are being pushed to the center of the circular table and cards are being tossed aside.

Rocco doesn't turn when a man with black hair places his hand on his shoulder.

The words he's saying to Rocco don't get any response out of him.

He studies Rocco's profile for a few seconds before he pats his chest and walks away.

Once he's gone, Rocco finally looks in my direction.

I raise my hand in a wave, but he doesn't acknowledge it.

The sadness cast over his expression answers the unspoken question on my lips. He doesn't see me.

Rocco may be staring right at me, but he's looking straight through me.

Chapter 26

Rocco

I sit on one of the folding chairs next to the poker table. I store all of it in the second bedroom and drag it out for poker nights with my friend, Dylan Colt, and whoever else we can round up. Tonight it was two guys Dylan met through work.

"You'd think you could let me win one time, you selfish son-of-a-bitch." Dylan slides into his suit jacket. "Would it be so damn hard to throw me a bone once in a while?"

I laugh at the expression on his face. It doesn't match his words. He's smiling through his faux anger filled rant.

"Fuck you, Dylan."

"Nice." He shoves a hand through his black hair. "I just handed over a thousand of my hard-earned dollars and this is how you treat me."

I made bank tonight, coming out of the game three thousand ahead of when I went in. Everyone else left with an empty wallet.

"You need to spend more time practicing on that app on your phone." I push on an empty glass tumbler. "Or you could quit the games."

"And miss seeing your beautiful face?" He pats my shoulder. "We need to hang out more than once a month, Rocco."

We do. Dylan is an old friend. Our stories date back to his law school days.

He's a divorce attorney; some consider him the best in the city.

"You know where I live." I sweep my hand in the air. "You're always welcome here."

He checks his phone before he pockets it. "We should head out of the city for a few days. Remember those trips to Vegas we used to take?"

How could I forget?

If Dylan had the time, he'd tag-along whenever I hit Sin City for a tournament. Those days are long gone.

"You want to go to Vegas?" I question with a lift of my brow. "Aren't you the guy who never takes a weekend off? I'm surprised you even show up for these games."

Chuckling, he shakes his head. "I am that guy. I have to go to Boston for a few days for work. You should come."

"And do what?" I move to stand. "Take notes for you?"

"We'll shoot some pool, eat a few good meals." His shoulders loosen. "Unwind. Decompress. Call it whatever the hell you want."

I call it bullshit because that's what it is.

He saw something in me tonight that no one else did. The ghosts of Dylan's past haunt him. Mine are less forgiving. They eat at my soul.

"You can break up with New York for a couple of days." He laughs to lighten the somber mood that's crept into the room. "When's the last time you got on an airplane?"

Two months ago. I flew to Los Angeles and hiked the canyons on my own for a week.

Dylan doesn't know. I don't run every last minute trip by him.

"I'm working on a new deal." I steal a glance at Dexie's apartment. "I can't leave the city right now."

His gaze wanders over my shoulder and out the window. "Does it involve the pink-haired bombshell I saw looking over here?"

"It's too early to say." I shrug. "Time will tell."

"Tell time to hurry the hell up." He taps me in the center of the chest. "At least one of us should be happy."

He's right, but fate has a hand in that and history has taught me, you don't get a choice over what life deals you.

***

You never know what's waiting for you just around the corner.

In my case, it's Dexie Walsh at midnight in a pair of white shorts, a blue T-shirt and red high heels.

I'm just exiting the bodega with a bottle of orange juice when I spot her sprinting past with a sketchpad in her hand.

"Fuck," she mutters under her breath when she comes to a dead spot. "No, no, please, no."

"Dexie?"

She whips around to face me. Panic washes over her expression.

"What's wrong?" I take a step closer to her. "Tell me what's wrong."

"My friend, Sophia, came over." She waves the sketchpad in the air. "She forgot this, so I ran down to give it to her, but the car was already at the corner, and by the time I got there, it sped away."

Her hair is falling softly around her shoulders. Her face has been scrubbed clean of the scant amount of make-up that she does wear. She's glowing in the pale light being cast on her from the bodega.

"I can get an Uber." I tug my phone from the pocket of my pants. "If you're lucky, the driver will beat Sophia to her own house."

Shuffling back and forth on her feet, she shakes her head. "I'll give it to her tomorrow. I can stop by her office on my way to work."

I scratch my chin. "You're not upset about the sketchpad?"

Her eyes wander to the entrance of her building. "I can't go home. I ran out so fast that I forgot my keys and my phone."

"If you need to make a call you can use mine." I offer it to her.

She looks at it, but her hands don't make a move. "I don't know my super's number. Harold's contact info is in my phone and that's in my apartment. Shit, shit and double shit."

"Triple shit," I chime in with a grin.

I should tell this gorgeous woman that I have Harold's number, but I conveniently forget to mention it. He's a friend of one of my uncles. I gave him a temporary job before he scored the one in her building.

"What am I going to do?" She rubs her hand over her eyes.

I rake a hand through my hair. I shouldn't. I fucking shouldn't suggest it, but I do because it's what I want most in my life at this moment. "Spend the night with me, Dexie."

Chapter 27

Dexie

I blink. I don't know what to say to that.

I can't tell if he wants me to stay with him because he's a good neighbor or if he's picturing us in his bed together.

I've pictured it. I'm doing it again now.

I shake the mental image of Rocco's head between my thighs from my thoughts and focus on the problem at hand.

"My apartment door is unlocked." I take the few short steps to my building. "My wallet and handbags are in there. Anyone can walk right in and take whatever they want."

I'm an idiot.

"Why did I forget my keys?" I pinch the bridge of my nose. "I put on my shoes and just took off after Sophia. I should have stopped to think."

I sense Rocco is behind me when I try and tug open the lobby door. It's locked. Why wouldn't it be?

I look over at the intercom panel. I could press any random button to ask one of my neighbors to let me in, but it would be futile.

The panel is broken. I know that because Sophia tried it earlier and it didn't work. She had to call me on my cell so I would buzz her in.

"Did you close your apartment door when you left?"

"I did."

"Your neighbors will assume you're fast asleep inside." His voice is soft and soothing. "I don't think there's much of a chance of anyone robbing you tonight."

That's easy for him to say. I could hear his keys jingling in his pocket when he walked toward me.

"I need to get up there." I glance up and down the sidewalk hoping that someone who lives in my building will show up.

"My offer is still open." He takes a step closer to me. "You can stay with me for the night and we'll get this sorted in the morning."

"I can't stay with you," I argue softly.

"Why not?"

He's persistent, but I know that it's not coming just from a place of desire. I see the concern that's blanketing his expression.

I could go home with him and stay up all night staring into my apartment. If I do that, I'll at least feel more secure in knowing that I'm not being robbed blind.

A burst of wind whips over the sidewalk sending a shiver through me.

Rocco reaches for my arm. "A storm is blowing in. You can't stand here all night. Come home with me."

I look at his hand. His touch is gentle, his voice comforting. I nod slowly. "I'll come home with you."

He leans forward, his breath whispering over my cheek. "You can trust me. You know that, don't you?"

I know I can trust him. What I don't know is whether I can trust myself not to climb into his bed.

***

I had no idea.

I had no clue that Rocco could see everything in my apartment so clearly. I left the overhead lights on when I slid my feet into the red heels in my rush to catch Sophia.

My entire living space is fully illuminated.

I glance at the half-eaten bowl of popcorn and the empty glasses next to it on the kitchen counter. My wallet and phone are right where I dropped them on my bed when I got home from work.

"You have a clear view into my life," I say under my breath.

I know he can't hear me. I'm alone in his living room.

I've seen this space before from my vantage point across the street. When we first walked in, Rocco directed me down a short corridor that leads to this room. A small kitchen is on left, and what I assume to be two bedrooms and a bathroom are to the right.

His furnishings are understated. The large brown leather couch against the far wall looks comfortable. A chair in the corner with a lamp perched above it would make an ideal reading nook.

The poker table and the folding metal chairs around it crowd the rest of the room.

I tug on the back of one of the chairs to bring it closer to the window. I sit so I can face my apartment.

"I see that you're already on surveillance duty," Rocco says as he rounds the corner.

I straighten and glance back to catch a wide grin on his face. He's changed his clothes. Dark sweatpants hang low on his hips and a white T-shirt covers his muscular chest.

I kick off my shoes and plant my feet on the windowsill. "I thought I should get comfortable since I'll be spending all night glued to this window."

He moves to stand next to me, his hands falling to his hips. "Are you hungry? Did you eat anything besides popcorn for dinner?"

It should bother me that he knows what I was snacking on earlier, but it's mildly endearing. "I'm good."

"There are some sandwiches in the fridge." He motions toward the kitchen. "Leftover pizza too. Everyone brings something to poker night."

I glance back at the table. It's littered with empty glasses, plates and poker chips. "You won, didn't you?"

"I always do."

I gaze up into his blue eyes. "I play."

"Poker?" A smile teases his mouth.

I nod, trying to hide the grin on my lips. "I'm good."

"I believe you." He reaches for the back of my chair. "Maybe one night when you're not staking out your apartment, you can join me for a game."

I bite back a laugh. "Maybe."

"I'll be right back." His fingers trail over my shoulder sending goose bumps crawling up my neck.

I hadn't thought about what it would be like when I accepted his invitation to spend the night here. I'm already squirming in my seat from his touch and we're just getting started.

Chapter 28

Rocco

I walk into my living room to the vision of a blonde-haired beauty staring out my window.

Her fingers are tugging on one of the pink-streaked strands of her long hair.

Guilt is still nagging at me. She doesn't need to be here. I could wake Harold and have him open the lobby door of her building for her, but I'm not selfish often.

I need this.

"I made coffee," I announce as I approach her from behind, not wanting to startle her.

Her shoulders still jump in surprise at the sound of my voice. "You did?"

I hand her one of the large white mugs before I pull a folding chair across the floor. I take a seat next to her, wrapping my hands around my mug.

She looks down at the cup she's holding. "I thought I smelled coffee brewing, but I didn't know if it was my mind playing a cruel trick on me."

I laugh. "It's real. Two sugars and a splash of cream for you; extra, extra hot for me."

She presses her lips together, her big brown eyes searching my face.

I offer her a quick explanation, so she doesn't assume that I spend all my time studying every nuance of her life. "I overheard you at Palla's the other day. I found some cream in my refrigerator. My brother takes his coffee with a load of cream and no sugar. He knows to bring it with him when he stops by for a coffee."

"You have a brother?" She flashes me a wide grin.

I blow on the coffee and take a small sip. "Two."

"Younger or older?" Her head tilts to the side.

I could get used to this; easy conversations over coffee late at night with the wind whipping the night air into surrender. It's soft howl the perfect backdrop to the darkness outside.

"I'm the oldest," I go on, "I have a sister too. She's the youngest."

"Four kids?" Her eyes widen. "What was that like growing up?"

Hell. My father could barely function after my mom died of cancer. He'd drag himself from his bed, go to work, rinse and repeat until he collapsed under the weight of his grief.

That's when Marti stepped in and fired the babysitters, worked out a childcare schedule with the Calvetti family and told my dad it was all right for him to love again.

He did.

He met a beautiful woman. Irena. She brought her daughter, Chloe, into our lives and our family was reborn with a framed picture of my mom front and center on the mantle over the fireplace.

Death stole Irena from us too.

"I have few complaints." I rest my hand on my thigh. "What about you? Brothers? Sisters?"

"A sister," she confesses softly. "She's younger than me."

My eyes catch on her bare legs. They're outstretched in front of her. Her skin is soft and tanned. It's flawless except for a small circular scar below her right knee.

"What happened there?" I reach out to touch it but stop myself. Instead, I circle my finger above it.

Her eyes follow the path of my hand. "What?"

"The scar."

She bends her knee. The movement shifts the fabric of her shorts to expose even more of her upper thigh. "It's embarrassing."

I swallow more coffee. "It can't be more embarrassing than how I got my scar."

Her brows rise in surprise as she studies my face. "You have a scar? Where?"

"You go first," I insist. "What happened to your knee, Dexie?"

She rubs her fingers over the jagged edge of the scar. "This was my last attempt to learn how to ride a bike. When I fell, my knee landed on a rock. The scar is a constant reminder that some people aren't meant for two-wheeled transportation."

"You don't know how to ride a bike?"

"Do you?" She shoots back with a grin, her hand flying in the air between us. "No, wait. Of course you do. You're one of those men who is amazing at everything, aren't you?"

Her eyes widen when her gaze drops from my face to my chest and then my lap. I've been semi-hard since I sat down next to her. It's her beautiful smile, those legs and the scent of her skin that has me all wound up.

"I'm amazing at the things that matter the most," I say in a low tone.

She brings the mug to her lips, but she doesn't take a sip. She holds it there in her shaking hands while her breathing evens.

I lean back in the chair and shift my focus from her face to her apartment.

I wanted her here. I've fantasized about her in my bed since the first night I saw her getting into hers.

I can't push. I won't, but being this close to a woman who isn't ready for me to touch her, is a sweet type of torture I've never experienced before.

Chapter 29

Dexie

I try to keep my eyes off the growing bulge in his lap.

My experience with penis size isn't extensive. I've had fun with a few men, but I doubt that any of them could compare with what's inside Rocco's sweatpants.

I shake that thought from my mind and take another sip of the coffee he made me.

I didn't expect it or the details about his family.

I half-expected him to try and use his masculine charm to persuade me to sleep with him.

He's more of a gentleman than I thought.

"How long have you lived in this apartment?" I glance at his profile.

We've sat in silence for the past fifteen minutes. A brief thunderstorm passed overhead, but only a sprinkle of rain fell before it rolled on.

"It feels like forever."

I expect a smile to follow those words, but the corners of his lips dip into a frown.

"I moved in when I was in college." He taps his bare foot against the edge of the windowsill. "I rented first and then when my landlord decided to sell, I bought it."

"You really like the neighborhood," I say jokingly.

When I first moved to Manhattan, it only took me a month to realize that avoiding midtown was a brilliant move.

The fact that I'm now living steps away from the busiest part of the city is ironic. The rent on my place was too reasonable to pass up though, so I deal with the cons to enjoy the pros.

"You get used to it." He exhales harshly. "I've lost count of how many people have lived in your apartment over the years."

His words lure my gaze back to my building. "You must have spent hours here watching your neighbors."

"No." His response is curt and quick. "You're the only person who has lived there that I've found interesting."

I'm skeptical.

He hasn't been shy about watching me. I haven't caught him peering at me under the raised corner of a closed blind or standing behind a veiled curtain.

There's been nothing subtle about his movements. He's been bold and unapologetic when he's stood at this window staring at me.

He reaches for my almost empty coffee mug, placing it next to his on the windowsill.

"There's something about you." He turns to face me in his chair. "It's not just the way you look or how you move. It's hard to explain. Fuck, is it hard to explain."

"Try," I say before I realize that the word has left my lips.

His stare burns into me. "It's soothing. I'd watch you talking on the phone, or sitting on the edge of your bed painting your toenails…"

"Pink," I whisper as I glance down at my feet.

"Pink," he repeats, a soft smile tugging on his lips. "The color of your T-shirt when you first saw me. You watched me unbutton my shirt."

I lower my gaze as I confess softly, "I did."

"You've been avoiding the window since the pitch session." He runs his gaze over my face. "Why?"

I wonder for a second if it's a rhetorical question because the answer is blatantly obvious to me. We've had this discussion.

Silence sits between us. He wants me to answer, so I do. "Things are different now. I know your name. You know mine. We may become business partners."

He nods. "The attraction hasn't lessened though. You want to stand over there and watch me."

My eyes flit to my empty apartment. "It was fun. I'd never done anything like that before."

His hands run over his thighs. "I haven't either. Watching you undress for me drove me fucking mad. There was one night. You were wearing a pale pink bra. I wanted you to invite me over. Do you remember?"

How could I ever forget? He tapped his bare chest twice and motioned that he wanted me. I turned him down.

"I remember," I admit.

His hand leaps from his thigh to mine. "I wanted you desperately that night."

I look down to where his fingers are splayed over my bare skin. His hand is large, his pinky finger brushing the hem of my shorts.

"You wanted me too." His words escape in a low growl. "You want me now."

"I want my business to succeed." My heart is hammering in my chest. "It has to be my priority."

His hand inches higher. "I understand that. I applaud it, but it's important not to lose sight of the big picture."

"What's the big picture?" My hand lands on his.

He squeezes the flesh of my thigh. "Intimacy and business can go together."

"What happens when they don't go together anymore?" I sigh heavily.

"We're adults." His voice is deep and measured. "We put the business first, and the past behind us."

I swallow, studying his face for something. He's so confident that we'll be able to drift into a solely business arrangement after we stop sleeping together.

"Are you still business partners with the woman you fucked?" I spit the words out in a hurry. "Or should I say women?"

His hand twists to grab mine, pushing it into my thigh. "It was one of my first deals. I was riding the high of making a small fortune in a short period of time. We celebrated our first million in her bedroom."

I listen even though I don't want to know more.

"We burned out quickly," he says hoarsely. "I haven't crossed that line since. I haven't wanted to until now."

A shiver runs through me. I want to cross it too even though we haven't defined it yet. I'm not even sure I'll partner with him, so what's the harm in taking all the pleasure I know he's offering?

"Let me make it crystal clear to you, Dexie." He shifts to face me. "Tomorrow, I want you as my business partner."

"And tonight?" I murmur.

"Tonight, I want to kiss you."

Chapter 30

Dexie

The deep timbre of his voice sends a wave of desire through me. His words spark a heated rush.

He cups my face in his hand and stares into my eyes. "Just a kiss, Dexie. I'm not asking for more."

He may not be asking for more, but my body wants so much more. I squirm in the chair, the metal squeaking beneath my movement.

"Fuck these uncomfortable chairs," he says sighing, his hands sliding to mine.

He glides to his feet, tugging me up along with him.

I stand on shaky knees, wishing that kiss would have happened.

I don't want that moment to be lost.

He looks down at me; his expression schooled in thought. "You're quiet. Tell me what's racing through that beautiful head of yours."

My gaze drops to his lips. "You want to kiss me."

"You want to kiss me," he repeats, his lips pulling into a soft smile.

I nod without giving it any thought. I don't want to think about *what ifs* and whether he's the best business partner for me.

"Now?" he asks as his hands slide up my body until one is wrapped around the back of my neck, the other resting on my hip.

I glance at the floor before I gaze back up and into his searing blue eyes. I reach forward to touch him for the first time.

My fingertips play over the muscles of his forearm, sliding up his bicep until I reach his strong shoulder.

I answer his question with a tilt of my head and a brush of my bottom lip with my tongue.

His breath escapes him in a heated rush as he leans forward and presses his soft lips to mine.

His hand moves from my hip to my back, luring me silently closer. I inch forward on my feet wanting to erase any distance between us.

He wants the same. He groans into my mouth when my lips part and I press my body into his.

I can feel his arousal. I know he can sense mine.

My nipples are hard, my core aching to be touched, to be taken in the same way he's taking my mouth.

I whine from the sheer need I feel.

He growls, his hands tightening, his kiss deepening.

The taste of his tongue on mine weakens my knees. I pull back from the kiss and look down.

"Dexie." My name is wrapped in pure desire when it leaves his lips. "That was…"

"So much," I whisper before he can finish. "That was so much."

He strokes the back of my head, his fingers trailing over the strands of my hair, luring my gaze up to his. "It was perfect."

138

The intensity in his face spurs a need inside of me. I want to pull his shirt over his head, tug down his sweatpants and drop to my knees. I want to pleasure him. I need to hear him come, feel him come because of me.

"Tell me what you want." He kisses me again, softer this time. His lips play over mine, teasing and biting, tempting me to confess my desires to him.

"You," I manage to say before I deepen the kiss.

He breaks it to pull back and stare into my eyes. "I'm all yours."

The intensity of those three words is almost too much, so I glance away, stealing a look in the direction of my apartment.

I stumble when I catch a glimpse of movement near my window.

Rocco's arms circle me as I let out a sharp gasp.

"What's wrong?" he asks, his breath skirting over the skin of my neck.

I wave my index finger in the air near his window. "It's...look...look over there."

He shifts slightly on his feet, his arms still holding me tight against him. "Is that..."

"That's Sophia," I say her name as she raises her hand in a wave. "Sophia is in my apartment."

***

I may not be able to hear a word Sophia is saying, but the expression on her face says it all.

She saw the kiss.

My best friend was a witness to my first kiss with Rocco.

139

I don't know how the hell she got into my building or why she's even there.

She waves her phone in the air in a gesture I think is meant to encourage me to call her.

I point at my bed, trying to get her to turn to see that my phone is behind her.

"I think she wants you to call her." Rocco pushes his phone at me. "Use this."

I take his phone and key in Sophia's number. Once I bring the phone to my ear, I motion for her to pick up.

"What the hell, Dex?" Her voice is panicked. "I thought you were missing."

I bow my head to hide my smile. I know she's serious. She's married to a man who writes detective novels for a living. Her brother-in-law and her father-in-law were both homicide detectives at one time.

Sophia always jumps from zero to sixty on the panic scale when anything is amiss.

"I locked myself out," I say quietly. "I left my keys in my apartment and my phone too. It's on the bed."

She glances over her shoulder. "Thank god you're all right."

"How did you get in the building?"

"One of your neighbors let me in on his way out. Gage something is his name."

I look at Rocco. He's busy tidying the mess on the poker table. "Go down to the lobby and wait for me, Soph. I'll be there in a few minutes."

"I want details, Dex." She sighs, pointing at me. "You were kissing your hot neighbor."

"Details tomorrow," I whisper. "I'll meet you in the lobby. Go now."

I end the call, waving her away with a brush of my hand.

Exhaling, I turn to Rocco. "Thank you for this."

He reaches for the phone, shoving it into the pocket of his sweatpants. "Is your friend all right?"

"Nosy, but fine." I smile. "I'm going to go meet her now."

He glances over my shoulder. "She's waiting for a second act."

I turn back to see Sophia still standing by my window. "Unbelievable."

Rocco laughs. "Curiosity is a powerful force. She's not budging until you're out of view."

I know he's right. Sophia isn't going to let up until she knows exactly what's going on between Rocco and me.

"I'll go."

"I'll walk you down."

"You don't have to do that." I tug on the bottom of my T-shirt. "I can handle it on my own."

"I know you can." He reaches forward to quiet my hands by covering them with his. "I want to walk you down."

Instant comfort washes over me. "Let's go."

Chapter 31

Rocco

"I'm Sophia Reese-Wolf." Dexie's friend shoves a hand at me. "And you are?"

The expectation in her voice is matched by the questions in her eyes.

I take her hand in mine, giving it a soft shake. "I'm Rocco Jones."

Her gaze volleys between Dexie's face and mine. "The poker player? You're not that Rocco Jones, are you?"

"I am," I admit, shoving my hand into my pocket.

She smiles, her head tilting to the right as she studies me. "You played poker with my brother-in-law a few times. Liam Wolf."

I consider him a friend. We met at the gym a few years ago. He's younger than me but much wiser than I can ever hope to be.

"You're married to Nick or Sebastian?" I ask because I'm honestly curious.

Liam has shared some details about his family, including the fact that he has two older brothers.

"I'm married to Nicholas," she says proudly, flashing her left hand in the air. "I can't believe you're Rocco Jones."

I laugh, scratching my upper lip. "It's good to meet you, Sophia."

She turns her attention to Dexie. "Let's go up to your place, Dex."

"I know you came back for this." Dexie shoves the sketchpad she's holding at Sophia. "I'm tired and it's way past your bedtime."

"I came back because I tried calling you six times and you didn't pick up."

Dexie rests her hand on Sophia's shoulder. "I'm sorry if I worried you, but I'm fine. It's late. We can talk about this tomorrow."

I've been leaning against the inside of the lobby door since we got here. No one has asked me to leave, so I've stayed in place.

"We should talk tonight," Sophia huffs.

"Tomorrow," Dexie insists, moving her hand from her hip to the handle on the lobby door.

I step aside.

"That's your car waiting by the curb isn't it?" Dexie nods toward the street and a black sedan that's been idling since we left my building.

"It's Nicholas's driver." She exhales. "I called him to bring me here."

"Go home." Dexie reaches for her friend's hand. "Go to bed. I promise we'll talk about this after we both get some sleep."

Sophia's shoulders soften. "Fine. I only came back because I was worried and I love you. I hope you know that."

"I love you too." Dexie takes her friend in an embrace. "Good night, Soph."

"Good night," she says to Dexie before she tosses me a look. "It's nice to put a name to the face, Rocco."

"It's been good to meet you, Sophia." I hold open the door as she passes through.

"Don't hurt her," she whispers under her breath when she breezes past me.

I watch her walk to the car. I'd stop her to say that I have no intention of hurting Dexie, but it's a promise I can't keep.

***

I follow Dexie into the lobby and watch as she presses the elevator call button. We haven't said a word to each other since Sophia took off, but I'm going on instinct here and assuming the silence is an invitation to join her in her apartment.

"I think I'll go up alone."

Apparently, my instinct doesn't know fuck all.

Disappointment rolls over me.

I don't know what the hell would have happened in my apartment if Dexie hadn't caught sight of her friend.

Judging by Sophia's parting words, my guess is that she would have hauled ass over to my building and knocked on every door on my floor until she found us.

She's fiercely protective of Dexie. I get it. I feel the same way and I barely know the woman.

"You're sure?" I ask because I'm selfish and I want to kiss her again.

Hell, I want more, but that's for another time.

Her head bows as a long exhale escapes her. "I'm sure."

I reach for her chin, tilting it up so I can look into her eyes before the elevator arrives and steals her away from me. "I'm glad you locked yourself out tonight."

A smile plays on her lips. "I am too."

"Can I see you tomorrow?"

She wraps her hand around my forearm. "I'm meeting Rhoda after work tomorrow to talk about my business."

I should care, but I don't. Whatever Rhoda proposes won't match what I have to offer to her.

"Don't commit." I drag my thumb over her bottom lip. "I want a chance to show you what I have to offer."

The elevator dings, announcing its arrival.

"I won't commit," she assures me with a gentle kiss to my thumb. "I'll see you soon."

I lean down to brush my lips over hers. "In five minutes."

"I need to sleep." The weariness in her tone is unmistakable. "Thank you again for everything, Rocco."

"Sleep well, Dexie."

Chapter 32

Dexie

My face scrunches. It has little to do with the bitter taste of the cocktail that Rhoda ordered for me.

It has everything to do with the offer she presented me with.

"I can't do it." I push the glass away from me. "I just can't."

Her arm is in the air waving the bartender over. The man hasn't had a second of rest since we sat down.

First, it was Rhoda's drink order. He made it once, twice and finally, the third time was the charm. Rhoda is a stickler when it comes to dirty martinis.

I decided that I wanted a soda water so I could keep a clear mind.

Rhoda frowned at that and took it upon herself to order me a whiskey sour. As the bartender made it, she told him a story about how it was the first drink she ever had.

Tonight will be the last time I ever have it.

"You need to remake this." Rhoda pushes my glass tumbler at the bartender.

He's handsome with black-rimmed eyeglasses, muscles for days and a voice that Rhoda can't seem to get enough of.

I get it. I like the rich baritone sound of it too, but I'd prefer if I had Rhoda's full attention so we could talk about the offer she threw at me right after I got here.

"You don't need to remake it." I clear my throat. "Can I get a soda water?"

"Sure thing," he says, tapping the palm of his hand on the top of the bar.

"Live a little, Dexie." Rhoda twirls the martini glass in a circle. "I can see the tension in your shoulders. A cocktail will chase that away."

My better sense will hitch a ride with it.

I don't need a drink. I need a business partner.

"Your offer is very generous, Rhoda," I say with a smile. "I'm just not in a position to give up that much equity."

She picks up the martini glass to raise it in the air. "From where I'm sitting, you're not in a position to keep that much equity."

Touché.

She has a point. It's valid, but if I hand over sixty percent of my company to her, she'll have controlling interest. I didn't work this hard to give up so much.

"I've already spoken with my suppliers and distributors. We can start production at several hundred units a day in a factory that I know does quality work." She winks at the bartender when he drops off my soda water. "Our handbags will be everywhere."

That's not my end goal.

I don't want to water down my brand so much that it loses its charm. Right now it's a boutique, personalized offering. I know that I can't sustain that.

147

If I want to keep it on the same path, I need to hire people who understand the materials and can craft them into the bags that I design.

I've never pictured an assembly line of my purses being made. To me, the vision has always been about a studio that houses women and men who are artisans. Together, we'd make the bags, using the same type of industrial sewing machine that I work on now.

In my wildest dream, I'd have a small storefront where I'd sell the finished products.

"What's Rocco offering you?" she questions before taking a sip of her drink.

Kisses that curl my toes.

I won't make that confession to Rhoda because it will cloud everything. Instead, I stick to the script I've been playing over and over in my head all day. "Rocco is still preparing his offer."

One of her long, red fingernails taps the bottom of her glass. "Rocco's hot as hell, isn't he?"

I scratch the back of my neck. This little black dress I chose to wear today is a new design from Sophia. I have no idea what the material is, but it's been irritating my skin since I put it on. "He's a good-looking man."

"Don't let that blind you." She grins like a Cheshire cat that just trapped a mouse. "I would never call him ruthless, but when it comes to business, he'll do what he can to seal the deal."

What happened between Rocco and me last night was all pleasure. There was no business involved.

I haven't heard from him since I got on the elevator in my building. He didn't try and influence me to skip this meeting.

"I'm not ready to seal the deal with anyone."

Rhoda lifts her eyebrows. "Fifty-eight percent equity?"

I shake my head. "I want controlling interest."

"Smart girl." She downs the rest of her drink in one large gulp. "I'm going to reconsider my position on this. When will Rocco's proposal be in your hands?"

"I'll let you know when I receive it and we can go from there."

She runs her hands over the crisp white blouse she's wearing. "You remind me of myself a very long time ago. I held tight to my convictions and look where it's gotten me."

I look down at the file folder that contains her offer. "We'll talk soon."

She glides to her feet, slinging her designer bag over her shoulder. "You have my number. Call me anytime."

As if on cue, my phone chimes.

I tug it out of my purse as Rhoda makes her way to the door.

I smile when I glance down at the screen and read the text. The words are simple, but the timing couldn't be more perfect.

Rocco: *I need your help. My grandmother's birthday is coming up. She needs a new handbag so show me what you've got.*

Chapter 33

Rocco

"Don't welcome her to the family, Marti." I squeeze my grandmother's hand. "She's a potential business partner."

"Or wife," she coughs out the word.

I arch a brow. "Business partner."

"What does this potential business partner look like?" She skims the palm of her hand over her hair. "Is she pretty?"

Beautiful. She's captivatingly beautiful.

I keep those words to myself and smile. "You'll see for yourself any minute."

Her gaze darts to the entrance of the restaurant. "I'll cook her dinner."

I look down at the empty bowl in front of me. Marti served me a healthy portion of risotto as soon as I sat down.

Food wasn't what I came here looking for, but I ate it.

I'll always eat what my grandmother cooks for me because I know damn well that a day will come when I won't have that privilege anymore.

"Dessert," I suggest. "Everyone loves your tiramisu."

"Your mama loved it most of all." Her smile softens. "She ate it almost every night when she was pregnant with you."

I'll never tire of her stories about my mom, even though I've heard each of them thousands of times.

"You miss her, yes?"

She's asked me that question already twice this week. It comes up multiple times every week.

My answer is always the same. "Very much."

"She'd want you to be happy, Rocco." A long sigh escapes her. "She'd want all of her boys to be happy."

We all are. Luke, my youngest brother, is a fireman. Nash runs his own ad agency. None of the Jones men are headed down the aisle, but there's still hope. Marti clings to it. She's always telling us that she wants to see at least one of us in a tuxedo taking our vows before she takes her last breath.

"Happiness comes in many forms." It's my standard line for her. It never appeases her, which is why her response to it is always the same. She counters with a comment about true love and how nothing can replace it.

"What about that form?" Her hand lifts in the air.

I turn in the direction she's pointing. Standing in the doorway of the restaurant is the woman I haven't stopped thinking about.

"That's her," I whisper. "That's Dexie Walsh."

***

"Your Rocco's grandmother?" Dexie narrows her eyes. "You're Martina Calvetti."

"Marti," my grandmother corrects her with a soft touch of her hand to Dexie's chin. "You'll call me Marti."

"Marti," Dexie repeats it back slowly. "I had no idea that Rocco was related to you."

"He's my daughter firstborn. He's my Gaia's son." Her hands leap to the middle of her chest. "God rest her beautiful soul."

Dexie's quiet for a moment before she looks to me and then Marti. "I'm sorry. I didn't know."

"It was a long time ago." Marti drapes her arm over Dexie's shoulder to comfort her. I've seen it before. My grandmother puts everyone's needs before her own; regardless of how well she knows them. "Time doesn't lessen a mother's loss, but it pushes me forward. I have a family to love."

Dexie nods.

"My grandson tells me you're here to talk business." Marti motions to the chair she was just sitting in. "You'll sit and talk. I'll bring you wine and dessert."

"You don't have to do that," Dexie says quietly. "A glass of water would be just fine."

"Water, wine and dessert." Marti tugs on a pink-streaked strand of Dexie's hair. "I like this. I thought about it, you know, at one time."

Dexie's face brightens. "You thought about pink hair?"

"Blue." Marti touches the front of her hair. "A streak or two, but what great-grandmother parades around looking like a peacock?"

"You'd pull it off," I interject. "Do it, Marti."

"You do it," she bounces the words back to me with a wink. "Don't color your hair blue, but take a chance. You know what I mean."

I don't have to read between those lines. She likes Dexie.

"Dessert, Marti," I urge her on. "We're going to talk business. You'll make that special dessert."

"I'll be back." Picking up my empty plate, she shakes her head. "There's more to life than business, Rocco. Don't you forget."

Dexie watches her walk away before she lowers herself onto the chair. "Your grandma is amazing."

I take the seat next to her. "I know it."

She pushes a strand of her hair behind her ear. She looks stunning tonight, dressed in a simple lacy black dress and yellow heels. The neckline of the dress dips low enough to reveal a small mole below her left collarbone.

"Are you looking for something premade for Marti or a custom piece?" She fishes in her red handbag. "I'll show you my available inventory. I have pictures of almost everything on my phone."

"You met with Rhoda."

Her hand slows. "I was with her when you texted me."

I assumed as much, which is why I was surprised when she answered my text quickly, agreeing to meet me tonight.

I told her I was here, at Calvetti's.

Before I could type out the address, she replied that she was on her way over.

"How did that go?"

She rolls her eyes. "The hot bartender got more of her attention than I did."

"Hot bartender?" A smile creeps over my lips.

Her gaze lifts to meet mine. "I have a feeling Rhoda chose that bar for our meeting because of him."

"Would you go back for another drink because of him?"

It's a question an insecure college kid would ask his girlfriend, so why the fuck is it coming out of my mouth?

"I might." Her eyes gleam. "There's something about nerdy, muscular types."

"Is there?" I lift both arms over my head, flexing my biceps. "Have I mentioned to you that I graduated summa cum laude?"

Her gaze skims my black T-shirt before her eyes land on my right arm. "You graduated with honors?"

"I was the captain of the chess team."

"You weren't." She shakes her head, her eyes now pinned to my left bicep.

"I was." I finally lower my hands to the table. "I ran the debate team too."

"Damn," she drawls through a grin. "I had no idea you were such a nerd."

I laugh aloud. "Now you know."

She lifts a finger to her chin. "Something tells me that there's a lot more I don't know about you and most of it will surprise me."

She's right. There's a lot she doesn't know about me. The surprise is that a part of me wants to tell her everything.

Chapter 34

Dexie

"You two are conspiring." Marti takes a seat next to me, across from her grandson. "What's going on here?"

The woman must be a mind reader because I was vigilant about not talking about her upcoming birthday gift whenever she was within earshot.

Rocco didn't specifically say that her gift is a surprise. I assumed that.

"Nothing gets past you, Marti." Rocco reaches to cradle her hand in his. "I heard you tell Gina that the strap on your purse broke again."

"That's not news to me." Her brows jump expectantly.

"Dexie makes beautiful handbags." He gestures toward the red tote hanging from the back of my chair. "I'm going to get you a new bag from your birthday."

My assumption about it being a surprise was way off base.

"No." Marti shakes her head adamantly. "I've had that bag forever. I'll tape it back together again."

"Tape," I say aloud, even though I didn't mean to.

Marti nods. "Tape does the trick."

Tape can destroy the structure of leather. It weakens it and fades the color.

"It's time to replace your bag." Rocco leans back in his chair. "Let me do this for you."

"Let us do this for you," I interject with a smile. "You can tell me exactly what you want, Marti. You design it and I'll build it."

That sets her up and out of the chair.

I look to Rocco for reassurance that I didn't just piss his grandmother off.

He smiles, giving his head a curt shake. "She'll be back. Give it a minute."

I take a sip of the water that Marti brought when she dropped off a piece of the most delicious tiramisu I've ever had.

I've never ordered dessert when I've dined here. I've also never met Marti. I've seen her bustling around the place, but until tonight we've never spoken.

"She likes you," Rocco assures me.

I should tell him that I like her too, but I stop myself. I don't know where I stand with Rocco. The kiss we shared last night was intense and the flirting tonight has been fun.

I still have an important decision to make regarding my business. After my meeting with Rhoda, I'm beginning to wonder if Rocco is the person who will help make my professional dreams a reality.

"This is it." The sound of Marti's voice startles me.

I look to my left to see her standing with a worn brown leather bag. She drops it in the middle of the table.

"I've had it for a long time." She lowers back onto the chair next to me. "A very long time."

I hear the quiver in her tone before I see the tears in the corners of her eyes.

This purse means much more to her than Rocco realizes.

"May I?" I ask as I inch my hand toward it.

She nods in silence.

I pick it up and examine the corners. If nothing has escaped through the small hole on the right side of the bag, I'd be shocked.

The gold-plated trim has worn away to reveal green metal underneath. Half of the clasp is missing and both straps are held onto the bag by duct tape.

"Can you make something similar, Dexie?" Rocco asks.

"I don't want similar." Marti squeezes my forearm. "I want the same."

I lock eyes with her, the depth of her pain is apparent. Her eyes are the same color as Rocco's and as clouded with unexpressed grief as his are.

His mother must have been an incredible woman.

"I understand," I say with a reassuring squeeze of her hand. "I can make something identical."

"Let her take it, Marti." Rocco's voice is steady. "Dexie will take good care of it."

"The best care," I reassure her with a smile. "I promise."

She dumps the bag onto the table, sending lipstick tubes, a smartphone and a mountain of papers flying everywhere. "Take it."

***

An hour later, Rocco and I are standing on the sidewalk outside my building. The Uber ride here from the restaurant was the first chance we had to be alone, and that was wasted because I had to take a work call. Rio Dirks finally got back to me about our upcoming photo shoot.

"Do you want to come up?" Rocco nods toward the door that leads up to his apartment. "You can teach me a thing or two about poker."

Or you could teach me a thing or two about great sex; correction, mind-blowing sex.

We haven't slept together, but the man exudes raw energy that is palpable.

I have to try and ignore it tonight.

"I have a lot of work to do." I push Marti's bag up my shoulder. "I've fallen behind lately. I have a few clients waiting for their orders."

"Understood." He shoves a hand into the pocket of his jeans. "Thanks for meeting me tonight and for taking such good care of Marti's prized possession."

I swallow. "I should probably go up."

He steps closer, his eyes skimming my face. "Kiss me goodnight, Dexie."

My teeth latch onto my bottom lip. A kiss with him makes me feel things I'm not ready to explore. It reaches beyond the physical need that it ignites in me. I like him. I want to spend time with him. I want to know him.

His hand leaps to my cheek. "What I'd give to feel you bite my lip like that."

A blush races up my skin. "One kiss?"

"For tonight," he whispers over my skin before he presses his mouth to mine.

158

The kiss is slow and sensual. The noise of the city filters away and all I can hear is the hammering beat of my heart.

His tongue parts my lips, the kiss deepens and I moan from the pent up need that washes over me.

That morphs into a soft groan when he slides his lips over my cheek and down my neck.

"Until tomorrow," he says in a low tone.

I stare at him under hooded eyes, my breath catching somewhere between my heart and my lips. "Tomorrow."

"You know where to find me if you *need me*." He pulls the last two words over his tongue in a raspy growl.

Exhaling, I step back and lower my gaze. I need him now. He has to know that. My kiss said it all.

"Goodnight, Dexie." He brushes his lips over mine for one last chaste kiss.

"Goodnight," I mumble before I turn and walk to the door.

Chapter 35

Dexie

I step into my apartment and flip the switch to turn on the overhead lights. Darkness has blanketed the city and if I'm going to get any work done tonight, I need as much light as possible.

The lamp in the corner just won't cut it.

Resisting the urge to look toward Rocco's apartment, I toss my bag, Marti's purse and my phone on my bed.

I stare at the worn leather bag that Rocco's grandmother took into her hands one last time before we left the restaurant.

When she shoved it back at me, I could see the tangled emotions on her face. I wish I knew more about the story attached to the purse, but I don't know her well enough to pry.

All I know is that she's expecting a replica of the bag for her birthday.

Turning on my heel, I head to my clothing rack and yank a short pink T-shirt dress from one of the hangers.

The constant itchy sensation from the lacy dress I'm wearing has reached the point of being unbearable.

I make a mental note to tell Sophia that it gets two thumbs down from me.

Making my way to the bathroom, I slide my hand over the back of the dress. I grab the zipper pull to open it.

The sound of my phone chiming stops me in place.

I sigh. I still haven't talked to Sophia about what she witnessed last night. She's called me four times today and sent me at least ten text messages.

I keep putting her off with the excuse that I'm up to my neck in work.

Marching back to the bed, I pick up my cell and scan the screen.

Rocco: *If you need help with that zipper, I'm right here.*

My head pops up to find him standing by his window with his phone in his hand.

I peer at him, a smile tugging on my lips. I fire a text back to him.

Dexie: *I think I can handle a zipper.*

His gaze drops to his phone. His fingers fly over the screen.

Rocco: *It's an open offer. I'm also great at braiding hair, painting toenails, staring at the most beautiful woman on the planet…*

I read the message twice, focusing on the last few words.

Another text appears.

Rocco: *I'm going to take a shower. Call me if you need ANYTHING.*

I press my phone against my chest as I steal one last look at him.

***

Three hours, and one cute red suede clutch later I type out an email to the client who has been waiting for this treasure.

It's done and as fabulous as I knew it would be.

I set it on the edge of my workstation and take a picture of it to attach to the email. The woman who ordered it lives in Boston and I want her to see it as soon as she wakes up tomorrow morning.

I press send and set my phone down.

I turn around to face my windows. As tempted as I was to try and catch a glimpse of Rocco after his shower, I resisted the urge.

Once I started sewing the purse, work consumed me.

It's always that way once a design starts taking its physical shape. I love the sprint to the finish line.

I take a few tentative steps closer to my windows, but Rocco's apartment is dark. It's so late that he must have gone to sleep.

I lean my forehead against the glass and draw in a deep breath.

The kiss we shared on the street sparked a need inside of me. It's different than what I felt when we kissed in his apartment last night. Each touch of his lips to mine fuels my desire for the man.

I gasp when a light pops on inside his apartment.

My heart rate kicks up when I spot him moving in his living room.

Turning to face me, I get my first look at him. He's wearing dark boxer briefs and nothing else.

His hair is a tangled mess. He looks just woken or just fucked.

We stare at each other, the energy flowing between us snapping with the raw power of want.

Life is about taking chances; diving off cliffs with the uncertainty of what's waiting but the belief that fate will be there to catch you.

I need to take this chance. I have to believe that whatever happens, my heart and my business will survive.

I lift my hand to the center of my chest, tap it twice through the thin fabric of my dress, and point at him.

An impossibly sexy grin takes over his mouth as he nods and motions with a curl of his fingers for me to go to him.

I do.

Chapter 36

Rocco

I descend the stairs two at a time, so I can reach the door before Dexie does.

I didn't waste a second after she motioned that she wants to join me. I brushed my teeth, slid a pair of gray sweatpants over my boxers and took off out of my apartment.

I swing open the door that leads to the sidewalk and find her two feet away.

Those red heels she seems to love are on her feet, and a thin pink T-shirt dress barely covers her body.

"Rocco," she says my name with softness in her tone. "I was going to buzz so you'd let me in. You didn't have to come down."

My building doesn't have a doorman. There's not a lobby in sight. A simple square intercom panel hangs on the exterior wall next to a glass door with a silver handle. Inside is a space large enough for two or three people to stand. The residents' mailboxes hang on a wall opposite the door.

There's one way to go when you enter the building and that's up. Carpet-covered stairs lead to the first floor and a landing that ties into the stairs that lead to the second.

I'm on the sixth.

"I want to walk up with you." I reach my hand out to her.

She moves closer, jingling her keys in her fingers. "I remembered this time."

I laugh as she brushes past me to enter my building. My cock has been hard since I saw her at her window.

She glances down at the front of my sweatpants. When she looks up, her cheeks have blushed a soft pink.

Dexie is the most seductive woman I've ever met. The way she dresses and her belief in herself speaks of a quiet confidence that's rare. I've never seen it in any of the women I've dated or fucked.

"You first." I motion to the stairs.

She brushes her fingertips over the hem of her very short dress. "Why don't you go first? I wouldn't want you sneaking a peek up my dress."

I let out a hearty laugh. "I thought you invited yourself over so I would look up your dress."

She cracks a wide grin. "You go first and we'll talk about what's up my dress after you make me a cup of coffee."

"Two splashes of cream and one sugar." I drop my hands to my hips.

She nods as her gaze slides over my bare chest. "Extra, extra hot."

***

The coffee mugs are empty, her red shoes are on the floor and her inhibitions are slowing slipping away.

We spent the last hour talking about her business and what she sees for the future of it.

Unless Dexie increases the price she's charging for her handbags, her business will never grow.

You can't make a product with as much precision and care as she insists on and make a fair profit on a bargain sales price.

Discussing the glaring inconsistencies in her business model will have to wait for tomorrow. Tonight I want to fuck her, not teach her the finer points of profit margins.

"What did you think the first time you saw me over there?" Her hand drifts in the air toward my window.

We're seated on the couch side-by-side. She stole one glance at her darkened apartment when she arrived. She hasn't looked in that direction since. Her focus has been solely on me.

I'm the luckiest man in the entire fucking world tonight.

"I saw you before you saw me," I confess. "I first saw you when Harold took you on a tour of the apartment."

Confusion knits her brow. "That was a Sunday night. It was raining."

"Your hair was wet." I reach for a pink strand of her hair. "Your clothes were wet."

Her hands leap to the front of her dress. "I remember that. I was wearing jeans and a white blouse."

And those red heels were on her feet.

The blouse was wet and sheer. I could make out the white lace bra she was wearing underneath. I don't know what the hell Harold had going on that night, but he couldn't tear his gaze from his phone's screen.

The most beautiful woman in the world was walking circles around him checking out the apartment, and he didn't once glance in her direction.

"I prayed that you'd move in." I shake my head with a chuckle. "The night you did, I watched from right here."

She finally turns to glance behind her at her apartment. "You started watching me the night I moved in?"

I nod when she locks eyes with me again. "A few nights later you saw me when I came home after a wedding reception."

"I'll never forget that night," she says softly. "I couldn't take my eyes off of you."

I slide closer to her, wanting her to know that this moves at her pace. I've been aching to kiss her since she arrived, but I didn't want to stunt whatever she's feeling by pushing her.

Her hands jump to my face. "Promise me that what happens tonight won't change anything between us. It won't impact our future business relationship...if I choose you, that is."

I smile at the addendum she tossed onto the back of her request.

I'll promise her the world right now because I want to kiss her more than I want my next breath. I want to touch her body, taste her cunt. I want inside of her.

"When we become business partners, we'll balance this with that," I say quietly. "One step at a time, Dexie."

Her thumb moves to touch the corner of my mouth as she repeats my words back to me, "One step at a time."

Chapter 37

Dexie

Rocco's mouth crashes into mine, and I whimper.

This is precisely what I wanted when I stood at my window and invited myself here.

I moan through the kiss when I feel his fingers on my thigh. I'm so wet. I know that my panties are drenched even though his lips have only touched mine.

His tongue parts my lips and finds my tongue, teasing and taunting me.

My body reacts to its need, sending my legs apart.

"Dexie," He breathes my name out in a groan.

It's so filled with pure want that I put my hand over his to slide it higher. I need him to feel what he's doing to me.

He growls when his fingertips skim over the rough lace of my panties. "Christ. So good."

He moves quickly, dropping to his knees on the floor in front of the couch. "I have to taste you."

Panic rushes over me. "No, we can't. No."

My hands fly in the air to try and motion for him to stand.

"Not here," I clarify because the look of pure disappointment on his face is almost too much. "Not by the window."

He stares into my eyes as his hands slide up to grab the waistband of my panties before he glides them down my legs.

They're tossed aside when his index finger runs over the length of my cleft.

"In my bed." His voice is dangerously low. "I need... I fucking need to taste your cunt."

My knees wobble as he hauls me up to my feet. He wraps an arm around my waist before he hoists me into his arms.

I stare into the most intense eyes I've ever seen as he pads down the hallway taking me to an experience I know I'll never forget.

***

My dress and bra are on the floor before he lowers me onto the bed.

A curtain covers the window, shielding our intimacy from anyone's prying eyes. I wanted him in the other room, but the thought of anyone watching us was too much. I couldn't do it. I can't do it.

There's just enough light filtering into the room that I can see all of him when he pushes his sweatpants and boxer briefs to the floor.

He's large and toned everywhere.

A happy trail leads to a thick, heavy cock between his legs.

He runs his hand over the length of it. "Do you know how long I've thought about fucking you?"

"Do it," I tempt him because my body is on fire. I need to come. I know that any touch from him will set me over the edge.

I don't care if it's his mouth, his fingers or that delicious cock that takes me there.

"No." Settling between my thighs, he shakes his head. "I eat first."

My back involuntarily arches when I feel the softest feather touch on my cleft. It's his lips and then his tongue darts out to circle my clit.

I drop a hand to his hair, winding my fingers between the silky strands.

This has been the fuel for my masturbation fantasies for weeks. I've hidden under the covers in my bed and gotten off to the mental image of Rocco licking me.

His mouth teases me, drawing sounds from deep within me that I don't recognize.

Each is met with a groan from him and a lash of his tongue against my throbbing clit.

I circle my hips, chasing the release I need so desperately.

My thighs tremble when I feel a finger slide into my channel. He moves it slowly, inching it back until another glides in with it.

I moan from the sensation of being taken like this. I'm so open and so vulnerable.

"So sweet," he whispers against my inner thigh. "Your cunt is so fucking sweet."

The words send me on a collision course with my need, and when his lips find my clit again and he sucks it between his teeth, I try to say his name, but the only thing that escapes me is a shuddering breath as I come hard against his mouth.

He licks me through my orgasm, his fingers gliding softly in and out, taking me from the high of one release, straight into the path of another.

"That was the most beautiful thing I've ever seen." He flicks his tongue over my sensitive clit. "I want that again."

I hide my face behind my hands. "I can't again."

Before I can process what's happening, I feel his lips on my cheek. "I wish you could see yourself."

I move one hand and crack open an eye to look at him. His hair is mussed from my fingers, his lips covered in the sheen of my release.

I reach up and run a finger over his mouth. "I've thought about you doing that."

His hand trails down my cheek to my left breast. He circles the swollen nipple with his fingertip. "You thought about me eating you?"

I close my eyes briefly against the rush of emotions. I've always fought hard to keep vulnerability at bay, but I trust him. For some reason, I trust this man to understand me. "I sometimes touch myself thinking about it."

"Show me."

"Show you?" I repeat his words back, unsure if he's suggesting what I think he is.

"Show me how you touch this beautiful body when you think about me."

I stare at him, unsure of what I can say to that. He just got me off and now his demand is one that I don't know if I can fulfill.

I've never touched myself in front of anyone. I haven't even done it with the lights on.

He slides away from me to open a drawer on his nightstand. I have no idea if he's reaching for a tube of lube or a vibrator to aid me in his request. That's not what's in his hand when the drawer closes.

It's a condom wrapper.

He rips it open, tossing the package on the floor at his feet.

He sheathes himself. His bicep flexes when he runs his hand over his cock.

"Show me." He moves between my legs, resting on his heels, his dick curling up toward his navel.

I look down at my pussy. It's still so wet from the combination of my need and his mouth. "Rocco..."

"Trust me." He reaches for my hand, kissing the palm before he lowers it to my stomach.

I push aside all of my reservations when I see the look in his hooded eyes. He's so desirous, so wanting of me.

I slowly glide my hand along my skin, until my fingers touch the top of my smooth cleft. I glance up to see his eyes transfixed on my hand, on each of my movements.

He growls when my fingers skim over my folds. His hand leaps to his cock when I circle the tip of my finger over my clit. I moan from the sight of his palm wrapped around his dick. It's primal and raw. His need to get off as desperate as mine was before he took me there with his mouth.

"You're so fucking perfect." He ups the pace of his hand when I draw fast circles over my clit with my fingertips. "That's it, just like that."

I mewl a response when he squeezes the tip of his cock.

"I can't," he says on a deep breath. "I fucking can't wait."

With those words, my hand is pushed aside, my legs spread by the width of his hips and he drives his big, beautiful cock into me in one long exquisite thrust.

Chapter 38

Rocco

I let go when I was inside Dexie in a way I never have before.

I fucked her hard, impulsively. My control snapped when she dug her fingernails into my shoulder. I went at her like a man who had been deprived of his life's sustenance for years.

When I came, it was with a sound so deeply rooted inside of me that she cried out.

She came too, her tight pussy pulsing around me as I rode her through her orgasm. As I dropped from my high, I fingered her clit, rubbing tiny circles around the swollen nub until she came again.

I stare down at my bed and the beautiful woman who is wrapped in my black sheets, her face buried beneath a mane of blonde and pink hair.

I want to wake her up by flipping her onto her stomach so I can eat her again, savoring the taste of her sweetness while she makes those hot-as-fuck noises that she made when I first brought my mouth to her pussy.

I scrub both hands through my hair.

What the fuck am I supposed to do now?

No tomorrow is ever going to be the same.

I've touched her. I've fucked her. I've watched her fall asleep.

I turn my back to her so I can catch my breath. My chest feels like it's collapsing in on itself.

"Rocco?"

I look to the heavens for help when I hear her whisper my name. I can't fall in love with this woman. That's never going to be my fate.

"Hey," I say quietly as I turn back to face her.

Her eyes lazily run over the length of my body. "You got dressed."

I snap the waistband of my boxer briefs. "Just these."

"You're wearing more than me." She kicks back the covers to reveal her beautiful, lush body.

I stare at it, taking in the flushed pink hue of her skin, her hardened nipples and the smooth plane of her stomach.

"Show me your scar, Rocco."

The scars that matter are inside of me, marring my heart. They've never faded. They never will.

I inch down the waistband of my boxers to run my finger over the scar on my left hip. "It's here."

She squints her eyes. "I can't see it. Come closer."

She urges me with a wave of her hand.

I take two steps closer to the bed until I'm standing right in front of her. "Look closely, Dexie. It's here."

She skims her finger over it. "I see it now."

I should launch into the story of how I took a flying leap off a swing at a playground after I snuck a can of beer from my dad when I was fourteen. I ended up on top of a broken soda bottle, the glass piercing my skin.

Six stitches and a promise to my dad not to drink anymore were the result. Marti had a few choices words for me that day too.

Dexie moves closer to me, her elbow resting on the mattress. "Come closer."

I move until my knees hit the bed. "I'm closer."

"Not close enough." Her fingers drift from the scar to dip below the waistband of my boxers.

I groan aloud when her hand circles my semi-hard cock. "Jesus."

"I told you that I thought about you tasting me." Her eyebrows perk when she tugs my boxer briefs down far enough to release my dick. "I thought about this a lot too."

I almost fucking drop to my knees when her perfect lips circle the crown of my cock.

"Yes," I hiss out, my hands tangled in her long hair.

She swallows me, working her hands over the length, twisting her tongue under the crown.

I fuck her mouth, slowly at first but when she squirms to the side of the bed and falls to her knees, I take everything I can.

With long, fast strokes I drive myself into her mouth.

Words are lost in my throat when I try to pull her back so I can come on her gorgeous tits, but she holds tight, determined to taste my release.

Lights flash behind my eyelids, the room quiets, and I lose all rational thought as I pump every last drop between her pink lips.

***

"An apple, six green grapes, and half a bagel. Your breakfast is served, Ms. Walsh."

She looks down at the plate I placed on her lap. "Rocco."

"I know you just woke up." I settle on the bed next to where she's sitting. "You start work in an hour so I thought I'd take care of the breakfast part of your routine. I'd like to help with your shower too."

Her eyes are still cast down when her head starts shaking. "I can't believe you did this."

Did what? I ran down to the bodega when she was passed out and bought her breakfast. I cut up the apple, removing the peel, washed the grapes and toasted the bagel.

"Your coffee is on its way." I tap the watch on my wrist. "I forgot to turn on the machine before I left, but you'll have a cup in your hand in two minutes."

"Rocco." My name is barely a whisper. "You are..."

Scaring the shit out of her.

I've watched her eat breakfast. I've been mesmerized by the care she takes in peeling an apple each morning. I've seen her count out six green grapes and toast half a bagel.

She must think I'm a fucking stalker.

"Dexie." I work on a swallow, scrambling to come up with the right words to tell her I'm not dangerous, just infatuated.

Her head pops up. The tears welling in her eyes cut me in two.

"I'm sorry if I overstepped." I swipe a finger across her cheek. "I noticed that you like these things for breakfast, so I wanted to..."

I'm stopped mid-sentence by the press of her lips against mine. She kisses me. It's soft and tender.

"No one has ever done anything like this for me," she whispers against my cheek. "Thank you, Rocco. Thank you."

I kiss the corner of her mouth, breathing in the sweet scent of her skin. Fuck the men who have woken up next to her in the past. She deserves everything. I only wish I was the man who could give it to her.

Chapter 39

Dexie

Who cries over an apple and a bagel?

Me. I did in Rocco's bed this morning.

I shake the unfortunate memory from my mind. After I shed a tear because he cut the peel off the apple just the way I like, I sipped my coffee and then left to shower at home before I dressed for work.

"What are you thinking about?" Sophia questions from where she's sitting on my couch. "Is it my spring collection?"

No. It's Rocco's cock.

I look at the window and his darkened apartment.

We haven't spoken since he walked me down to the lobby door of my building this morning. We kissed and said our goodbyes before he took off down the street in running gear.

"Do you want another cup of chamomile tea?" I change the subject effortlessly. "Have you warmed up at all?"

Sophia ran two blocks through the rain earlier to get here. It was a brief shower, but she got caught in it on her way here from the subway stop. When I opened my apartment door her red T-shirt and shorts were dotted with raindrops.

"I'm better." She wraps her bare legs in a blanket she tugged off my bed. "I could use a glass of water."

I go to the sink to fill a glass, stealing another glance at Rocco's apartment.

It's still dark.

"Dex," Sophia calls out. "You haven't talked much about the pitch session lately. You said you had two investors interested. You must have news to share about a potential deal."

I down the glass of water in my hand in one large gulp. "Both investors are putting together an offer. I'll make my decision once I have all the facts in front of me."

I refill my glass and grab another for Sophia.

"Tell me about the investors." She tucks the blanket tighter around her legs. "What are they like?"

"Rich," I joke as I shove the glass of water in her hand.

She takes a sip. "That's why they're the investors and you're the investee."

I plop down next to her, tugging on the hem of the yoga shorts I'm wearing. "I hope I make the right decision."

"You will, " she assures me with a squeeze of my knee. "You made the right decision when you kissed Rocco."

I see the smile on her face out of the corner of my eye. "I thought you might have forgotten about that kiss."

"That kiss was hot-as-hell." She fans herself. "The man wants you, Dexie."

I can't argue that. He wanted me last night and this morning again before I went to work.

I had to stop him, or I know that my day would have been spent in his bed.

"He's good for you," she announces. "I think he's the best thing that's happened to you since you moved to Manhattan."

I'd agree, but I've accomplished so much since my move from Rhode Island. Rocco and I spent one night together. I can't let what I'm feeling for him overshadow everything else that's going on in my life.

"He's a nice man," I say. "I don't know him that well, Soph."

"Give it time." She leans her head back on my couch. "A year from now you'll be Mrs. Rocco Jones. Mark my words."

"I'll be Dexie Walsh," I correct her with a grin. "Hopefully, by then I'll be working full-time for myself and my handbags will be the toast of the town."

"You'll make it happen." She snuggles under the blanket. "When you do, Rocco will be right there beside you."

***

"That's him, isn't it?" Rocco jerks a thumb toward the bartender.

The bartender.

I'm back at Rhoda's favorite bar because she asked me to join her for a drink after work. I showed up on time, but she bailed with an apologetic text message. Her last meeting of the day ran long so when Rocco called me to ask if we could meet up, I told him to head over here.

"That's who?" I try to brighten the mood when he sits next to me.

He huffs out a laugh. "Is this punishment for disappearing on you last night?"

It's not.

I was hoping that he'd get home before I went to bed, but I passed out right after Sophia left.

When I woke up this morning, Rocco wasn't at his window. I had a marketing meeting at eight, so I didn't want to text him for fear of waking him.

Instead, I showered, dressed, ate my usual for breakfast, and took the subway to Matiz.

"They make a great whiskey sour here." I smile. "It's Rhoda's favorite."

He leans in for a quick peck on my cheek and a squeeze of his hand on my bare knee.

"I like this dress." He looks over the white sundress I'm wearing. "You're the sexiest thing I've ever seen."

I should argue that point with him. He's dressed in a suit today. It's a gray suit with a black button-down shirt underneath. He looks gorgeous.

"What can I get you?" The bartender interrupts our mutual stare-fest.

Rocco looks at the glass of soda water in front of me before he turns to face him. "I hear you're known for your whiskey sours."

"Among other things," he says before he looks at me. "I was about to ask you if you were here the other night before my phone rang, so…"

Rocco squeezes my knee again, but this time his hand lands on my thigh.

"I was here." I nod.

The bartender leans his elbows on the bar. "I knew it. Who could forget that face? I'm Zeke."

I look at Rocco. He cocks a brow as his hand inches higher, moving closer and closer to my pink lace panties. Thankfully, Zeke can't see a thing from where he's standing. I do a quick glance around the interior of the bar to make sure no one is watching us.

"Your name is Dexie, isn't it?" Zeke asks with a slight hint of hesitation in his tone. "I heard the woman you were with the other night call you that."

I rub my index finger over my bottom lip. "That's my name, yes."

Zeke smiles. "It's a great name. Unique enough to be unforgettable."

I look past him to a large glass shelf behind the bar. It's home to an eclectic mix of items including a few books, several candles and an antique wooden chess set.

I glance at Rocco with a smile before I turn my attention back to Zeke. "That's a beautiful chess set. Do you play?"

Zeke glances over his shoulder. "I do. Do you?"

"Do you, Dexie?" Rocco asks as his hand crawls up the skin of my inner thigh until his fingers brush against my core. "You like to play games, don't you?"

My breath catches in my chest when he slides his fingertip along the seam of my cleft through the lace. "Sometimes."

Zeke's gaze volleys back-and-forth between Rocco and me. "I have a feeling you two will be leaving here together tonight."

"You can bank on that." Rocco continues to tease me through the lace of my panties. "I'll skip the whiskey sour. Bring me whatever beer you have on tap."

I watch Zeke walk away.

"Are we here so you can tease me?" Rocco runs his lips over my cheek. "You made me hard."

I gaze down at the outline of his erection in his pants. "I came here to talk business."

"If this is what being in a partnership with you is like." He reaches for my hand to cup it over the front of his pants. "I'll give you whatever the hell you want. Show me where to sign on."

Chapter 40

Rocco

I was tempted to haul Dexie over my shoulder caveman style to carry her up to my apartment.

Watching her talking to Zeke back at the bar was entertaining.

I suspect he would have asked her out if I wasn't parked on the stool next to her, but that's not what got under my skin and made me hard as nails.

It was the fact that I could feel her getting wetter and wetter under my touch.

She was reacting to my hand on her body.

The faux flirting was cute, but that's all it was. She didn't want him. She wants me.

I push my key into the lock of my apartment door and push it open with my foot. I'm clinging tightly to her hand.

"I'm not offering you anything right now." I toss my jacket and keys on the chair in the corner before I head down the hallway to my bedroom. "If you want a coffee or a peeled apple, or whatever the hell else, it has to wait until I fuck you."

Her mouth drops open.

"Stay like that and my cock is going to be sliding between those lips in less than a minute."

"Yes, please," she mewls, backing up against the wall just outside my bedroom door.

My hands are on her, pushing the dress over her head, unclasping the pink lace bra she's wearing.

I drop my mouth to her left nipple and bite it.

She moans and wiggles her hips. "I'm so ready, Rocco."

I know she is. My hand found its way up her skirt in the Uber on the way here. I draped my suit jacket over our laps and fingered her slowly while I kissed her.

I was careful not to take it too far. I didn't want her to come there. I want her to come wrapped around me, with my dick buried in her sweet cunt.

Her hands are on the buttons of my dress shirt as she stands in front of me dressed only in panties and black high heels.

I reach for the hair on the back of her head. I fist it in my hand and give it a sharp tug.

She gasps aloud, her hands clawing at the front of my shirt.

I lick a line from the bottom of her chin, down her neck to between her tits. Her right breast gets my attention this time. I swirl my tongue around the nipple, teasing it until I know it has to be aching.

"I'll come from that," she whispers. "I need to come."

I'm on my knees before she can say another word. I push the lace aside, dive my tongue between her folds and eat her until she squirms against my face in an intense release.

***

I pick up the condom packages from the bedroom floor.

Two. I fucked Dexie twice. Once after I'd eaten her to orgasm and then again an hour ago when she woke up.

She's in the shower now, washing that beautiful body of hers. I wanted to invite myself along for the ride, but I let her be.

"Rocco?"

I turn to see her standing near the doorway to my bedroom. She's nude. A white towel is draped around her shoulders.

My hand jumps to my chest. "Wow."

She gives me a rake from head-to-toe. "Wow."

I didn't bother getting dressed since I planned to hit the shower as soon as she was done.

She leans her bare hip against the doorjamb. "Can I ask you something?"

The pull to walk toward her is strong, but I stay in place, my hands dropping to my hips. My cock is hardening. How could it not when I'm staring at her? "Anything."

Her gaze darts to the hallway. "I went to get a glass of water when you were asleep. I couldn't help but notice the paintings in the hallway. I saw them the last time I was here, but I really looked at them this time."

I stare at her. I've had too many women to count in my bed but not one has mentioned any of the artwork in my apartment.

"The one at the end of the hallway is a Brighton Beck." Her eyes widen. "That's a Zeus Barnaby right next to it, isn't it?"

Anyone who has taken a tour of the Met in the past decade would know Beck's work. Zeus Barnaby is a mixed media artist. His work was included in a recent show featuring up and coming artists of New York at the Museum of Modern Art.

The fact that she knows both artists shocks the hell out of me.

There's a surprise at every turn with her.

"It's a Zeus Barnaby." I smile.

"It's amazing." She tugs on her earlobe. "Your hallway is a mini museum."

It's the tip of the iceberg.

Art is one of my guilty pleasures.

"We should take a tour of the Met." I haven't made that suggestion to anyone in a long time.

Her mouth softens into a smile. "I'd love that."

"Today." I approach her. "We'll go to the Met and then spend the rest of the day here."

Her gaze drifts to the bed and the tangled sheets. The room smells like sex. Our sex.

"I can't, Rocco."

"It's Saturday." I stand in front of her, disappointment ripping through me. "You don't have to work."

She tilts her head to the left. "I have to work on a few handbags today."

"Take a break for dinner," I suggest with a raise of my brow. "I'll come over and cook for you."

Her top teeth drag over her bottom lip. "You'll cook for me?"

"I'll be there at eight." I reach for her hand. "Come back to bed with me for an hour before you leave."

188

She takes my hand to guide my fingers down the side of her hip. "You only want an hour?"

"Hell, no." I grab her waist and pull her body flush against mine. "At least give me two. Forever isn't enough time with you."

Chapter 41

Dexie

Forever isn't enough time with you.

Those words have been replaying in my thoughts all day. They were spoken in a moment of passion.

He didn't mean it. Rocco doesn't honestly think that forever isn't enough time with me.

It was his cock talking, not his heart.

"Ouch!" I let out a sigh when I look down at my index finger.

A drop of blood is pooling on my fingertip. It serves me right for working with straight pins when I'm daydreaming about the most incredible man I've ever met.

I stand and cross my apartment to run my finger under cold water from the kitchen faucet.

Movement in Rocco's apartment catches my eye. I stop, hoping to share a moment at the window with him.

It's not meant to be.

Marti is with him. Her hands are cupping his face, a soft smile graces her lips.

It's a moment in time between a loving grandmother and her grandson.

I glance back at her purse. It's sitting on the wingback chair waiting for my attention.

I brush the blood on my finger away with a tissue from the box on the kitchen counter and I head straight for Marti's bag.

I sit with it in my lap, looking over the leather.

The interior is stained. Holes have worn into the bottom of it.

I run my hand along the inside, feeling the silk, wondering how many years the purse has hung from Marti's shoulder.

I stop when I reach a zippered compartment. The bump within is obviously something Marti overlooked when she dumped her purse on the table at Calvetti's.

I open it and reach inside.

It's a small yellowing card. Curiosity bites at me so I open it.

I read the words that are handwritten inside.

Happy Mother's Day Mama!

I know you'd never treat yourself to this, so I got it for you.

Thank you for helping with Rocco, Nash and baby Luke.

You're the best in the world.

I'll love you forever and ever.

Your Gaia

Gaia.

Marti's daughter. Rocco's mom.

I look over at the window. Rocco and Marti are nowhere in sight.

I stare down at the purse, tears pricking the corners of my eyes.

I understand now why Marti is so attached to this purse. Her daughter gave it to her.

The significance of what I'm holding in my hands hits me full force. I tuck the card back into the compartment, zip it shut and hug it to my chest.

***

"Who taught you how to cook?" I look down at my almost empty plate. Rocco prepared a delicious meal of salmon, risotto and a side of roasted vegetables. He paired it all with a bottle of white wine.

If that wasn't enough, he brought me a vase filled with pink daisies.

"Marti," Rocco answers succinctly. "All of her grandchildren have to spend a summer at the restaurant when they're fourteen. She uses that time to teach us the basics of cooking and the facts of life."

I laugh. "Marti taught you the facts of life?"

"I stopped her after she brought up a bird and a bee." He winks. "I told her I didn't need the lesson, and she told me to always use a condom."

"Your grandma is the best grandma in the entire world."

I haven't brought up the card I found in Marti's purse. It wasn't mine to see and I'm not sure how Marti would feel about knowing I've seen it.

He takes a swallow of wine from one of the coffee mugs he found in my cupboard. After he arrived at my apartment two hours ago, he ran back and forth between my place and his gathering all the cooking utensils and pans he needed to make us dinner.

"Tell me about your family."

"There's always been just the three of us. My mom, Raelyn and me."

"Raelyn is your sister?"

I nod. "Younger sister."

A question is there in his eyes. I know it's about my dad so I answer before he can ask. "My dad left right after Raelyn was born. We met up with him a few years ago but there was too much water under the bridge."

The details about the meeting don't matter. It was in a diner on a Sunday afternoon. He wasn't looking for daughters. His next meal was his only concern. We left with Raelyn in tears and my anger boiling over.

I change the subject easily. "Did I tell you how handsome you look tonight?"

He looks down at the dark jeans and white button-down shirt he's wearing. "You like this look?"

"This look." I circle my finger in front of his face. "You're the best looking man I've ever met."

"I've never met a woman like you." He rakes me over.

He did the same when he arrived. I showered after I finished working and slipped into a strapless black maxi dress. The only thing I'm wearing underneath is a pair of black panties.

My hair is in loose curls around my shoulders. I opted for mascara and a thin coating of pink lip gloss that is now mostly on the rim of my coffee mug.

"A woman with pink-streaked hair?" I ask.

He slides his chair closer to me. We're seated at the small dining room table that came with the place. The two chairs are mismatched; both are wooden, but mine is painted blue and Rocco's is white.

"A woman who is fiercely independent, determined, sexy-as-hell." He pushes my hair back over my bare shoulder. "You're strong and soft at the same time."

I like that he sees me that way. I've worked hard to take care of myself. I haven't relied on anyone in years. Whatever my future holds it's because I've taken the steps to get myself there.

"I know this is officially a date." He drags my hand up to his mouth to feather kisses over my palm. "I want to talk business for a few minutes."

A grin tugs at my lips. "I think we can fit in some business before the pleasure."

"Here?" He tilts his chin toward my bed.

"There." I point at the windows and his apartment across the way. "I don't want all of your neighbors to watch us."

"We'll talk and then we'll have dessert at my place."

"I'm dessert?" I ask hopefully.

His lips skim the sensitive skin of my inner wrist. "You're my dessert. There's a piece of tiramisu that Marti made just for you in my fridge."

Words don't come. I don't know how to respond to that. It's an innocent offering, but it feels like so much more to me.

"I've looked over your business model, Dexie." He holds my hand to his cheek. "You've done remarkably well for yourself."

I'm proud of what I've accomplished. I haven't had a lot of time to devote to my handbag business, but I've been lucky. Customers have found me, I've made them happy and word-of-mouth has helped my business grow slowly every year.

"I know that quality is important to you." He sighs. "In a perfect world, you'd hire a few people just like you and they'd spend their time creating your designs. That's the vision, right?"

I nod. "In a nutshell. I know that it won't be an easy task to find the right people or purchase the materials at a lower cost, but it's crucial that each bag is made with the same care I would give it."

"One of the things I always tell entrepreneurs is to talk to someone who has earned the success they want." He closes his eyes briefly. "I made a call and if you're willing, I'd like you to meet with Suzanne Belese."

"Suzanne Belese?" I gulp down a breath.

"I take it you know who that is?" He laughs.

Suzanne Belese is living my dream. She and her husband started their handbag design studio in their garage in Los Angeles ten years ago. I saw an article about them online and since then, I've followed their journey closely.

Within the past few years, they've opened up boutiques in L.A. as well as Las Vegas.

"She'll be in New York next week." His hand leaves mine and trails up my arm to my bare shoulder. "I think she can offer some insight into what your next steps should be."

"I'd love to meet her," I say trying to disguise the giddiness in my tone.

"I think you have the beginnings of a great thing here." He glances over at my workstation. "I want to help. I'd love to partner with you on this, but I think it's prudent for you to consider every avenue available before you make a decision."

"Thank you." I rest my hand on his cheek. "I won't decide anything until I've spoken with Suzanne."

"You'll tell Rhoda to back off?" He narrows his eyes. "She's going to try and steamroll you into an offer, but I have no doubt you'll stand your ground."

"I can take care of myself." I flex my arm. "Strong and soft, remember?"

"I'll never forget." He leans forward to brush his lips over mine. "I'm craving my dessert. Come home with me."

Chapter 42

Rocco

A sweeter dessert has never touched my lips.

I've spent the past hour tasting every inch of Dexie's skin. I savored the most delicious parts of her; the skin at the back of her neck, the palms of her hand and the wetness between her legs.

I'm inside of her now. Fucking her in long, easy strokes.

Her legs are wrapped around me, her hands drifting through my hair.

"You're beautiful," I whisper against her lips.

"You are," she sounds back with a whimper.

I up the tempo, driving into her a touch harder, a measure deeper.

"Like that," she says through a moan. "I want that."

I want it too. I want to thrust into her so furiously that she'll feel me for days.

Her chest heaves with quick, labored breaths.

I felt it before when she was wrapped around me this morning. She's close; so close.

"Come." I arch my back away from her so I can watch.

I want this imprinted on my mind forever. I want to remember what she looks like when her desire engulfs her and nothing exists but the wave of pleasure she's riding.

Her pretty pink lips part. The sound that rolls off her tongue is like my drug. I drill into her taking her over the edge until I feel the velvet grip of her cunt as she pulses around me.

***

I tie off the condom and toss it in the wastebasket in the bathroom.

My reflection in the mirror says it all.

My face is flushed, my hair a tangled mess from her needy hands and my bottom lip swollen from the bite of her teeth.

I don't recognize myself.

The man staring back at me is a stranger.

His blue eyes have a life in them that I've never seen.

I look down, unsure if I can handle this. If I can handle the rush of emotions that hits me like a tsunami every time I see her.

"Rocco?"

Her breathy voice flows over me like warm honey. It coats my soul.

"I'm in here," I call back. "I'll be right out."

"Or I can come right in." She marches in, pushing her hair back from her face.

Her cheeks are red; her lips more swollen than mine.

Her hair is a tousled halo around her angelic face.

"Can we take a bath?" She drops her hands to cover the mound that I want to drop to my knees to feast on.

Tasting a woman has always been my pleasure, but Dexie is addictive. I want more.

"Of course," I say, brushing a strand of her pink hair away from her face.

"Do you have bubbles?"

"Bubbles?" I huff out a laugh.

Her head tilts to the right. "Bubble bath, Rocco. Do you have any?"

I 've never sat my ass in the tub. I'm a shower guy. "I can't say that I do. I can go down to the bodega and grab a bottle."

"I have the best lavender bubble bath at my place." She smiles. "Samples are one of the perks of working at Matiz. I'll run and get it."

I eye her up. "There's no way in hell you're going over there looking like that."

She spins in place, slowing to shake her luscious bare ass at me. "This is New York City. No one will notice that I'm nude."

"I'll go," I offer. "I'll throw on some pants. I'll be back before you can say, 'I can't help but stare at your cock, Rocco.'"

Her hand leaps to cover her eyes. "Busted. How am I supposed to not stare when it's right there?"

I run my hand over my now erect penis. "I wasn't complaining. I'm glad to know you find me stare-worthy."

"You're every woman's dream."

I don't want to be any woman's dream but the one standing in front of me.

She shakes off her last words with a wave of her hand in the air. "I'll grab my keys. The bubble bath is right next to the bathtub."

I move closer to her, watching her eyes widen with each of my steps.

"Be gentle, Dexie." I run my finger over her chin, tilting it up so her gaze meets mine. "I've never had a bath with a woman before."

Her brows pinch together. "You haven't?"

I've never felt my heart ache in my chest like this before either.

I push the words back deep inside of me with a brush of my lips over hers. "I'll get my pants."

"I'll get my keys. Hurry back, Rocco."

I will. A minute away from her is a minute too long tonight.

Chapter 43

Dexie

I stare out the window of Rocco's apartment and into my own.

I smile when the overhead lights pop on and I see him standing in the doorway.

He's wearing a pair of black long shorts and sandals on his feet. His chest is bare.

I watch him disappear out of sight into the bathroom. He emerges seconds later with the bottle of bubble bath in his hand.

I wave, hoping to catch his attention.

I don't, but something in my apartment does.

It's a picture in a silver frame that sits on the small round table next to my couch.

He picks it up and stops in place.

It's a picture of my small family. My sister, Raelyn, is on the right, dressed in a light blue dress, her long blonde hair blowing in the wind. I'm to the left in a dark blue dress that Sophia made just for that day. I bunched my hair on top of my head.

In the middle is the woman who has inspired me endlessly.

The smile on my mom's face overshadows the cap on her head and the gown draped around her.

The picture was taken just a few months ago on the day my mom graduated from college. Blue sky and trees border us.

My mom became a registered nurse that day. I couldn't have been prouder of her.

She sacrificed her dreams to nurture her daughters' dreams. She worked three jobs to support us when we were children.

That day all of her hard work was finally rewarded.

I tap my fingers against the glass of Rocco's window, knowing that he can't hear it.

I lean closer to the glass and whisper words I'm not ready for him to hear. "I think I'm falling in love with you."

He turns suddenly to face me. The frame held firmly in his strong hand.

"I know I'm falling in love with you," I say quietly when his eyes find mine.

He sets the frame down in its spot on the table along with the bubble bath and approaches the window with steady, even steps.

I study him in my apartment, wondering what it would be like to wake up next to him in my bed every day.

He points at the white dress shirt I'm wearing. It's the only thing I'm wearing.

I found it slung over the back of a chair in his bedroom.

I brought it to my nose and inhaled. The scent of his cologne comforted me so I slipped it on, silently conspiring how I was going to steal it so I could sleep it in every night when I'm not here.

His lips curve into a smile.

I smile back, urging him with a finger curl to come back to his place.

Just as he nods, a sound pulls my gaze back over my shoulder.

It makes no sense.

I glance back at Rocco in my apartment and then toward the door of his apartment.

I pause when I hear the jingle of keys.

I step closer with the click of the lock turning.

Just as I reach the door, the handle moves and it flies open.

I step back to avoid being hit.

"Jesus." A man's voice hits me full on as I lock my eyes on a broad chest covered in a lightweight navy blue sweater.

I look up into a face that resembles Rocco, but it's younger. This man's hair is a shade lighter, and his eyes are the same sea blue as the man who lives here.

I stand in stunned silence with the stranger staring back at me.

"Who are you?" I finally take a step back.

He cocks his head to the left, taking me all in. "I'm Luke."

"You're Rocco's brother," I state, not ask.

"You're ..." he starts before he looks past me to the dimly lit apartment. "Alone? Where's my brother?"

I jerk my thumb behind me. "He ran to get something."

He takes a step into the apartment, dropping a black duffel bag on the floor. "He left?"

I tug the shirt closer to my body. He can't see anything he shouldn't, but I still feel exposed. My sex hair and the fact that I'm wearing his brother's shirt is a dead giveaway for what I've been up to. What Rocco and I have been up to.

"Just for a minute." I tap my toes against the hardwood floor.

"He's an idiot."

Heavy footsteps precede the next words. "I'm not an idiot, Luke."

Relief rushes through me when I hear Rocco's voice and see him round the corner from the stairs.

"You left this beautiful woman all alone." Luke points at his brother. "What the hell did you need to get that took you away from her?"

I laugh aloud.

Rocco's lips cut into a smile. "Lavender bubble bath."

"Who the fuck are you and where's my brother?" Luke peers past Rocco's shoulder.

"Inside." Rocco directs him into the apartment with a hand on his back.

Seeing them side-by-side is remarkable. There's no doubt they're brothers. They share the same smiles. Luke is an inch or two taller than Rocco, and his hair is shorter, but their jawlines are identical, and the way they narrow their eyes is the same.

I move to the side when Rocco closes the apartment door, locking it again.

"My roommate has some people over." Luke picks up the duffel bag. "I was going to crash in the spare, but if you need me to go, I'll hit up Nash's couch."

Rocco looks to me. The hesitation in his eyes tells me everything I need to know.

"You'll stay," I say even though it's not for me to decide. "I should get home."

I should be disappointed over the missed bubble bath, but I'm not. I shove my hand at Luke. "I'm Dexie..."

"Walsh." Taking my hand in his, he finishes for me. "Luke Jones."

I smile knowing that Rocco must have mentioned me to him.

He turns his attention to his older brother. "Gina told me about Dexie. She can't keep a secret. You know that."

My smile dips into a frown. "I'll get dressed and leave you two to visit."

"I'll walk you out." Rocco shoots Luke a look. "Don't go to bed. I need a word."

"One word?" Luke jabs his finger into Rocco's shoulder. "Since when are you a man of few words?"

"Make some coffee." Rocco swats Luke's hand away. "Make mine..."

"Extra, extra hot," Luke and I say in unison.

"I like you." Luke wags a finger at me. "I like the pink hair too."

Tonight didn't turn out exactly the way I want, but I can't complain. I got a small glimpse into Rocco's life and I like what I'm seeing.

Rocco's heart is as big as the ocean when it comes to his family. He's everything I could ever want in a man. I can only hope I'm everything he wants in a woman.

Chapter 44

Rocco

I gaze out the window at Dexie. She ducked into her bathroom when she got home. She's still wearing the shirt that she put on earlier. It's my shirt.

I like that she's going to sleep in it.

She blows me a kiss and I pretend to catch it in my fist before I touch my hand to my lips.

Her palm lands on the glass of her window. I follow her lead and plant mine on my window.

With a soft smile, she backs away and moves toward the lamp.

Darkness follows and I know that she's crawling into her bed.

"I didn't mean to chase her away." Luke approaches me from behind. "I would have gone to Nash's place if I had known."

I'm always Luke's first choice when he needs a place to crash for the night or a few days.

Last year he took up residence in the spare room for six months.

I didn't complain.

I miss having my family here. We used to gather for poker nights to eat pizza. We'd play with nickels and dimes.

My door was always open if anyone needed a place to stop to get a coffee or a word of advice.

So much has changed.

"It's fine," I say brusquely, turning to face my younger brother. "What's going on with you?"

He's showered since Dexie left. He's shirtless now too. The tattoos on his chest are an homage to the two most important women in his life. Gaia and Irena.

The ink is his remembrance of them both, even though he was only a few months old when our mother died.

"Work." He shrugs. "I work too fucking much."

He's twenty-nine-years-old and single. Work should consume him. Being a firefighter keeps him out of trouble. He got into his fair share when he was younger, but he's leveled off. The paycheck that comes with responsibility set him on the right track.

"Forget about me." He rests his hand on my bare shoulder. "Let's talk about Dexie."

I shake my head. "We're not going there."

"Why the fuck not?"

I scowl. "She's fun. We're having fun, Luke."

"You don't have lavender bubble bath fun with women." His hand dives to the waistband of his sweatpants. "This is different."

I don't respond to that. I can't explain what's happening between Dexie and I to him because I can't make sense of it.

"Gina said you're going to partner with her." He clears his throat. "She makes designer handbags. That's right up your alley, isn't it?"

I laugh at the jab. "Fuck you."

"You want to make her dreams come true," he states with a tilt of his chin. "I saw the way she was looking at you. You're already her hero."

I feel like I'm racing down a hill at full speed with no brakes.

"We're done talking about Dexie." I brush past him. "Did you put the coffee on?"

"No coffee for me." He shakes his head. "It'll keep me up all night."

That's why I'm craving a cup.

Sleep is my enemy. It brings an arsenal of nightmares with it.

"Have you talked to Pop lately?" I ask because our dad was due back from his honeymoon two days ago. "I tried calling, but it went straight to voicemail."

"He's a newlywed." He winks. "Give him space, Rocco."

I have been, but I know my dad better than anyone. Life has taken its bitter toll on the man. He's chasing his happy-ever-after with April, his third wife.

My prayer as I watched him marry her was that he'd take his last breath before she draws hers.

That's his wish too.

"Are you headed to bed?" I want his company, but I know his schedule.

"If I hit the hay now, I'll get a good three hours." He drops both hands to his hips. "I pulled the early shift."

"Don't let me keep you."

He nods his chin at me. "It was good to see you happy tonight. I hope I see more of that."

I turn back to the window. Happiness comes at a price I'm not sure I'm willing to pay.

"Night, Rocco." He starts toward the spare room. "Go to bed before I get up."

Crawling into my bed with its sheets scented with the fragrance of Dexie Walsh is all too inviting. I follow my brother out of the living room, walk into my bedroom and slam the door shut.

If I can't have her in my bed, I can chase away the nightmares with a dream about her.

Wishing won't make it so, but I can sure as hell try.

Chapter 45

Dexie

Standing at my window, I let out an audible sigh.

"What's wrong?" Sophia glances at me from where she's sitting on the couch. "Did the fish not sit well with you either?"

I steal a glance at her over my shoulder. "What?"

She rubs her stomach. "I think the fish tacos we had for lunch were bad."

They were fine and delicious.

I sneak one last peek at Rocco's window, but he's not there.

"I can make you a tea." I walk to the kitchen. "Peppermint tea always settles my stomach."

"Can you make it iced?" She fans herself. "I think your air conditioner is down again."

The roar of it blowing should have been her first clue that it's working just fine. "You're just too hot to handle."

She barks out a loud laugh. "Look at me. I look horrible today."

She looks incredible. We're both dressed down in red T-shirts and white shorts. I accused her of planting a hidden camera in my apartment when she picked me up for lunch.

We look like twins save for the color of our hair and eyes and her height advantage.

"Get my mind off my nausea." She watches me make her iced tea. "Do you have a deal in place yet?"

"I have something better." I plop two ice cubes into a tall glass. "I have a meeting with Suzanne Belese."

"Seriously?" Her voice rises in pitch.

"Super seriously," I toss back. "I'm meeting her sometime this week. Rocco arranged it."

She waits for a beat before she says a word. "He's good for you, Dex."

"He's good to me," I correct her with a smile. "He's looking out for my best interests."

"Nicholas was the same way with me." She leans her head back on the couch. "He did everything in his power to make me happy. He still does."

I've never felt envious about Sophia's relationship with Nicholas. I was there when they navigated their way through the beginning of their love story. She wanted nothing to do with him. He wouldn't give up.

He won her heart and now that smile on her face is permanent.

"Rocco doesn't want me to make the wrong decision about who to partner with." I pick up the glass of iced tea. "Suzanne's path is the one I want to follow, so I think talking to her will put things into perspective for me."

"It will." She nods. "You'll tell me everything she says, right?"

"You know I will," I say as I hand her the glass. "I need you to help me with something today."

"Anything." She takes a long sip of the cool tea. "This is so good."

I point at Marti's handbag on the wingback chair. "That is a treasure, and I want to do something extra special for the woman it belongs to."

Sophia's gaze follows my finger. "That's a treasure?"

"It is." I pat her knee. "I have an idea of what I want to do with it. I'm hoping you can add your two cents because your opinion is priceless to me."

"I'm in." She takes another swallow. "Let's get to it."

***

The warm breeze blowing over my back is distracting. The sight of Rocco in a pair of black running shorts and no shirt is mind-numbing.

He's sweaty and listening to something with a catchy beat judging by the way he's hopping in place on the sidewalk in front of his building.

His phone is strapped to his bicep. Ear buds are settled in place.

The man is turning the head of every person who passes by him.

I can count myself among them.

It's late afternoon and I'm on my way home from Sophia's apartment.
After we brainstormed about Marti's purse, we took the subway to Sophia's place.

She ordered me to put on this beautiful backless pink shirt.

It's made of the softest material and the tie around the bottom is knotted at waist level.

It's sexy, flirty and a perfect match for my white shorts and red heels.

I smooth my hand over my hair.

Just as I'm about to tap Rocco on the shoulder, he pivots in his running shoes to face me.

He tugs his ear buds out and flashes me a killer smile. "I knew you were close. Sweet summer roses. That's what you smell like."

He smells like every fantasy I've ever had.

"You look incredible." He taps his bottom lip. "I bet you taste even better."

Two women stop to gawk at him. He's oblivious. His gaze is pinned to me.

"I'm going to shower and then let's get a drink." He cocks a dark brow. "Are you game for that?"

Since my master plan for tonight was working on a handbag, I opt-in with a nod of my head. "I'll meet you back here in twenty minutes."

"Fifteen." He leans forward to give me a chaste kiss. "I'll be right back."

I wave my smartphone in the air. "I'll call ahead and tell Zeke we're on our way."

"No Zeke," he growls, his hand grabbing my hip. "I want you all to myself tonight."

I want him all to myself tonight, and every night to come.

"No Zeke," I repeat back with a brush of my tongue over my bottom lip. "Just you and me."

The pad of his thumb follows the path of my tongue. "Perfect."

Chapter 46

Rocco

I let her win.

I bought Dexie a glass of white wine at a bar down the street from our buildings, then I brought her back to my apartment, stripped her naked, fucked her raw and bathed her skin in soft kisses while she settled.

Once she was ready, I grabbed a deck of cards and a bag of pretzels.

We played a makeshift game of Texas hold'em on my bed.

I wore the black boxer briefs I have on now. She's wearing a smile and one of my T-shirts.

"Look at all my pretzels." She picks them up and tosses them on the white blanket we're sitting on. "Tell me you at least tried to win."

I lean back on one hand. "You want me to lie to you, Dexie?"

She blows out a breath between her lips. "Not lie. Call it role play."

I huff out a laugh. "You won all those pretzels because I was so distracted by your smile."

Her hand moves to cover her mouth. "My bottom teeth aren't perfectly straight."

They're not. One overlaps another by a touch. It's barely noticeable, but I've saved to memory everything about her.

"Your teeth are perfect."

"Your teeth are perfect," she volleys the words back to me. "You're kind of perfect in every way."

If that were true, my life would be much easier.

I pick up a pretzel and take a bite.

"You're eating my winnings." She slides to her knees to gather the pretzel sticks into a pile. "That's going to cost you."

I pick up two more and eat both slowly. "What's the price I need to pay?"

Her hand slides over her hair. "Will you braid my hair?"

"Turn around."

I run my hands through her thick hair, tugging at the strands to straighten them.

"Is Luke coming over tonight?"

I yank on her hair, pulling her head back so I can run my lips over her cheek. "Why?"

She laughs. "I like him."

"You like him?"

Her hand reaches up to cup my cheek. "I like that he's someone who has known you for a long time. He must have a lot of secrets to tell about you."

"Tell me a secret about you." I move back to separate her hair into three sections with my fingers.

Her breath hitches. "A secret about me?"

"One secret."

She leans forward. "I was engaged once."

My hands drop from her hair. I was expecting a confession about a drunken phone call or an obsession with chocolate, not this.

"When?" I ask the question in a low tone.

"Five years ago." She holds up her hand, her fingers moving in the air. "Our engagement lasted a month. I broke it off."

"Why?"

She looks up at the ceiling. "He wanted me to change. He wanted the pink streaks and the nose piercing gone before the wedding. He told me that I should have grown out of that phase by the time I was twenty-one."

"How old are you?" I don't give a shit what the answer is. I know she's younger than me. "Twenty-seven." She steals a glance at me. "You're thirty-five."

"You know this…" I trail my words.

"The internet."

I get back to work on her hair, smoothing the strands between my fingers. "He's a fool."

"I was for thinking I could spend my life with someone like him." She sighs when I start braiding her hair. "I'm glad I realized before I said 'I do' to him."

I finish the braid, listening to the steady rhythm of her breathing.

"Your turn." She spins around to face me.

"I tried braids once." I shove both hands through my hair. "It's not a look that works for me."

She laughs. "You didn't."

I shrug a shoulder. "I didn't."

"Your secret, Rocco. What is it?"

I have a million and a spare. I choose a simple one that I know will keep a smile on her beautiful face. "I told Luke to sleep at Nash's place tonight if he needs a place to crash."

"Nash?"

"My other brother."

She nods. "Why did you do that?"

"Three words." I lean forward to press my lips to hers. "Lavender bubble bath."

She jumps to her feet, sliding the T-shirt over her head.

I rake her from head-to-toe, sending my cock into an instant erection.

"What are we waiting for?" She hops off the bed.

I'm on my feet too. "You're driving this train. I'm just along for the ride."

She claps her hands together. "I'll draw the bath. You get a candle."

"A candle?"

She stops just inside the door of my bedroom. "A warm bath, your arms wrapped around me and candlelight. That's all I want tonight."

"I'll get the candle," I say without pause because it's all I want tonight too.

Chapter 47

Dexie

"Rocco had only good things to say about you, Dexie," Suzanne Belese sips on the expensive cocktail she ordered the minute she sat down.

I'm on my second soda water. I took the afternoon off for this meeting. My boss at Matiz was more than happy to grant my request seeing as how the sales numbers for the lipstick campaign I headed are through the roof.

I have only good things to say about Rocco too. This morning I blew him a kiss through the window as I was readying for my day.

We've both been busy with work for most of this week. Our last chance to be together was the night we shared a candlelit bath.

"Your work is beautiful." She points a red fingernail at my white clutch purse. "Your attention to detail makes all the difference in the world."

The compliment is genuine. Every Belese bag I've ever seen has been crafted with the utmost care.

"Thank you," I offer with a smile. "That means a lot to me."

"Rocco was kind enough to fill me in on your vision for your venture." She leans forward so her elbows are resting on the white linen tablecloth. "I think there's room in the market for Dexie Walsh."

I think there is too. I know it's crowded and finding a customer base won't be easy, but I'm more than willing to do whatever it takes, short of selling my soul, to make it happen.

"Rick and I started Belese in our garage." She smiles with the mention of her husband's name. "We were both working full-time jobs. We'd get home after a long day and head straight to the garage. We were sleep deprived for years."

"It paid off," I point out with a lift of my glass in the air.

She holds up her glass to tap it against mine. "In spades."

"What do you think set you over the edge?" I sigh. "When did you make the leap from your garage to a boutique?"

"When we found the right partner," she says with ease. "That was the key for us. It took a few years but once we found someone who saw the value in what we were doing, we hit the ground running."

It was the answer I was expecting, so I push harder. "That's when you scaled up?"

"We did that over time." Her nail taps a beat against the tablecloth. "Some people see us as an overnight success, but that's not our story. There were years of sacrifice and hundreds of mistakes, but we never quit. We knew that if we kept at it, word would get out and Belese would become a brand to be reckoned with."

I nod, taking in every word she's saying.

"We wouldn't be where we are today if we didn't give up some control." She shakes her head slightly, causing her short brown curly hair to bounce. "Your specialty is designing handbags. Your talent is undeniable, Dexie. Focus on that and your future business partner will focus on everything else."

She's right. I've wanted a partner for years. Rhoda and Rocco are both giving me a chance to have that.

"Some people are good at this." Her fingers run over the edge of my clutch. "Others are good behind the scenes. Don't get caught up in trying to master it all."

"I just want to pick the right partner." I laugh. "Why does choosing a partner feel like the biggest decision of my life?"

"Because it is. You're trusting another person with your life's work." Her hand brushes over mine. "All you have to do is find someone who sees what you're bringing to the table."

I gaze down at my red skirt.

My heart tells my perfect partner is Rocco, but the fear of what happens if our personal relationship ends scares the hell out of me.

"I'm not too late to join in on the fun, am I?"

My head pops up at the sound of Rocco's voice.

"Rocco!" Suzanne glides to her feet. "I'm so glad you could make it."

They embrace as I push to my feet.

"Dexie." Rocco turns to me, brushing his lips over my cheek. "How are you?"

Surprised. When we exchanged text messages earlier, he wished me well at the meeting and told me that his day was jam-packed with meetings of his own.

He gestures for Suzanne and me to sit. We both lower in our chairs across the square table from one another. Rocco pulls a chair from another table to sit between us.

"I love this place." Suzanne twirls her finger in the air. "Lucien has been nothing but gracious."

I sit back and watch a wide grin slide over Rocco's lips. "I told you one day I'd own a place like this."

When Suzanne asked me to meet her at Sérénité, a French restaurant on Tenth Avenue, I searched it out online. The reviews are stellar and I'm all for taking a journey into a new culinary adventure.

I had no idea Rocco owned it.

"We haven't ordered lunch yet." Suzanne glides her fingers along the arm of Rocco's gray suit jacket. "You'll join us, won't you?"

There's a familiarity between them that's undeniable.

His eyes skim her face before he looks at me. "I'd love to."

He motions the female server over and in perfect French he orders something that sounds like heaven on a plate.

"Tell me what's happening with you, Rocco?" Suzanne's fingers play with the heart-shaped gold pendant around her neck. "Any exciting news to share?"

I wait with bated breath to hear the next words out of his mouth, hoping that it will be something romantic about him seeing a woman across a starry sky and falling breathlessly in love with her.

"Pop and April tied the knot."

"They're married?" Her mouth curves into a grin. "I didn't think your dad would take the plunge again after Irena died."

April? Irena?

If I felt I had a foot planted firmly in Rocco's inner circle, I just got my ass kicked out of it by Suzanne.

Her and Rocco are clearly old friends or more.

"Has it been two years since Irena passed?" Suzanne's brow knits into a frown.

"Three." Rocco hangs his head.

Suzanne reaches over to squeeze his hand. "If he's happy, I'm happy too."

Good for her, because I'm confused as hell.

Suzanne must read minds because she squares her attention on me. "I'm sorry, Dexie. Did we lose you? We were just talking about Rocco's dad and his second and third wives. Don't mind us."

I stare at her, trying to absorb everything she just said. I've never felt more like a third wheel.

Grabbing for my clutch, I stand. "I'm going to use the ladies' room. If you'll both excuse me."

Rocco pops to his feet, reaching for the back of my chair as I stand.

"Let's get a bottle of that Shiraz you sent for my birthday last year." Suzanne waves at the server. "We'll toast to Pop's happiness."

I try to steady my thrumming heartbeat with a hand to the middle of my chest. "I'll be right back."

No one responds as I turn and walk away.

Chapter 48

Rocco

"Walk with me?" I pose the question to Dexie on the sidewalk outside of Sérénité. We had a delicious meal, talked about Suzanne's daughter and finally rose from our chairs when Rick called to ask me where the hell his wife was.

I had texted him on my way to the restaurant to see if he wanted to join in on the fun.

He declined because he's rooting around Brooklyn looking for a space to open the next Belese boutique.

"I'm headed to Bryant Park," I add as I watch her scan the traffic passing us by.

She was mostly silent through lunch, picking at her food and checking the screen of her phone at regular intervals.

I know her work at Matiz was on her mind because she excused herself a second time to take a call from Shona.

Something else was gnawing at her.

"I'll walk with you." Her gaze drops to the watch on her wrist. "I need to stop at my office before I go home."

It's an out she needs, so I don't question it.

She tucks her clutch under her arm and starts in the direction of the park. She's dressed exquisitely today. The red pencil skirt she has on hugs her ass like a glove. The black blouse she's wearing is sheer and cut low in the back. The black heels on her feet are sky high.

I'd label the look conservative except her black bra is visible and her hair is tumbled in sexy waves.

She gave me the once-over when I got to the restaurant. I appreciated it. I dug out a suit for this along with a black dress shirt.

My goal wasn't to impress anyone but Dexie.

The sounds of the city surround us. Horns honking, people talking, and sirens in the distance.

"How do you know Suzanne?" She turns to look up at me as we slip past a woman pulling a wagon filled with groceries.

"I went to high school with her husband." I inch to the edge of the sidewalk when a group of uniformed school kids pass us with two adults in tow. "I'm their daughter's godfather."

"They have a daughter?"

"Holly." I tug my phone out of the inner pocket of my suit jacket, slowing my pace as I pull up a picture of Suzanne, Rick and their seven-year-old daughter. "Take a look."

Dexie stops to gaze at the screen of my phone. "She's adorable."

"She's a handful." I squint against the late afternoon sun.

"Did you partner with them on Belese?"

It's a direct question I knew was coming. I offered the capital Rick and Suzanne needed a few years ago to take Belese to its own boutique, but they shot me down.

Rick's a proud man and a good friend. He didn't want to tarnish the friendship by dragging business into the mix.

I respect their decision.

"No," I say firmly.

She sets off down the sidewalk again. I fall in step beside her.

"Did talking to Suzanne help you in any way, Dexie?"

She glances up at me. "I think so. It all comes down to making the right decision about who to partner with."

"That's an easy decision." I slow as we stop for a light. "Choose me."

"It's not that easy," she says as she stares across the street and the people huddled there waiting to cross. "I have to think about the future. I can't make my decision based on what I'm feeling in the present."

The light changes and she moves to take a step onto the street. I stop her with a hand on her hip. "What are you feeling in the present?"

She pauses, her eyes cast down. "Overwhelmed."

I slide my arm around her, tugging her closer to me as people brush past us on their way to live their own lives. "Talk to me, Dexie."

Her eyelids flutter as he looks up into my face. "I need to think about what's best for Dexie Walsh."

"You or your business?"

"Both."

I'd tell her right now that I'm the man for her in every capacity, but those words don't leave my lips.

"Put your offer together, Rocco." She takes a step away from me. "I'll have Rhoda's final offer soon and then I'll choose."

"I will." I reach down to run my hand over her chin. "Are you okay?"

A soft smile graces her mouth. "I'm good."

"You're remarkable," I correct her with a press of my lips to hers. "Come to my place after you go to Matiz."

She waits for a beat before she answers. "I have to work on a handbag tonight."

"I'll meet you at the window at midnight to say goodnight."

"How can I say no to that?"

"You can't."

She peers up at me. "I'm going to walk over to Matiz now. You'll find your way to Bryant Park alone?"

She can't know the spear that runs through me from her words.

Alone. I go to the park alone every week. I was hoping today might be different.

"I know the way," I assure her with a nod of my head. "I'll see you at midnight."

"Midnight, she repeats back before she sets off across the street.

I stand in place, watching until she seamlessly blends into the pedestrian traffic. When she disappears from view, I finally exhale.

Bryant Park waits so I set off toward it, alone again.

Chapter 49

Dexie

The Internet holds at least some of Rocco's secrets.

Irena Jones, mother and wife, was taken too soon.

Those are the words of the archived obituary I found online for Rocco's stepmother.

When I sat behind my desk at Matiz, I flipped open my laptop and typed the name Irena Jones in the browser.

She was in her mid-fifties when she passed three years ago. There's no explanation for how she died or the mention of a charity that those grieving can donate to in lieu of flowers.

It was just a simple posting on a website about a woman who had a loving husband, a daughter, and three stepsons, Rocco Jones included.

I cued up a search for April Jones, but the results ranged from a porn star to a pop singer, so I gave up.

If Rocco wanted me to know details about his family, he'd share them.

It makes sense that Suzanne would know all about it since they've been friends for years.

A loud bang from the apartment across the hall draws me to my feet. I've been home for almost three hours. After Matiz, I stopped to buy some fruit and then took the subway here.

Rocco wasn't home then and since I've been focused on working on Marti's handbag, I haven't glanced back to see if he's there.

I do now.

He's standing in front of his window, wearing the same gray suit he was earlier.

I look down at the cut-off denim shorts and black tank top I'm wearing.

We're as mismatched as we can be.

I move closer to the window, knowing he's staring right at me.

My phone chimes so I pick it up from my bed and scan the screen.

Rocco: *I've never seen a lovelier vision than this.*

Words hold so much power.

I type back a response.

Dexie: *Was the suit today for me?*

He tilts his head back, eyeing me from head to toe before he looks back at his phone.

Rocco: *You like me in a suit.*

"I like you every way," I say to myself.

Rocco: *What was that? What did you say?*

I look up and shrug.

Rocco: *Tell me what you said.*

I look directly at him, catching his gaze. I tempt fate. "I love you in every way."

His eyes narrow before he casts his gaze down to his phone.

Rocco: *I didn't get it. Say it again. Slowly this time.*

A knock at my door startles me. I turn back. "Who is it?"

No one answers, so I type a message to Rocco.

Dexie: *Someone's at my door. I'll be right back.*

Another knock greets me on my way across my apartment. I ignore the chiming phone in my hand because I'm ninety percent sure Sophia will be standing on the other side of the door. My time with Rocco will come to an abrupt end once she plops herself on the couch.

I know she wants to talk about her spring line. She sent me at least ten text messages today about it.

"You have zero patience." I swing open the door on a sigh.

It's not Sophia.

"Patience is a virtue. I don't do virtues."

I smile at the handsome brown-haired man standing in front of me. My eyes flit across his chest and toned stomach under the unbuttoned white dress shirt he's wearing. "Can I help you?"

"You can tell me that you forgive me." His hands drop to his hips and the waistband of his faded jeans. His feet are bare.

Where the hell did he come from?

My phone starts ringing. I glance down to see Rocco's name lighting up the screen. I turn back to the window, but he's not there.

"I don't know you." I point out to the guy in front of me. "What could you have possibly done that I need to forgive you for?"

He glances down at my phone. "You should get that, no?"

I dart a finger in the air. "Give me a minute?"

"I've got all the time in the world." He leans against my doorjamb.

I slide my finger over my phone's screen just as the ringing ceases. I look up at the green-eyed stranger in front of me. "I'm busy. I think you have me confused with someone else."

"I don't," he says with a confident nod of his head. "I live across the hall from you."

The loud bang I heard. He's here about that.

I should point out that it's only one in a series of noises that have been coming from his apartment the past few weeks.

A ding from the elevator lures both our gazes down the hall. Rocco marches out once the doors slide open.

"Dexie," he says my name in a heated rush. "What's going on?"

"My neighbor…" my voice trails when I realize I don't know the man's name.
"Gage Burke." He shoves a hand at me. "It's nice to meet you."

"Dexie." I take his hand. "This is Rocco."

Rocco doesn't offer his hand. Instead he wraps an arm around my waist. "Is there a problem, Gage?"

"A thousand of them at last count." He huffs out a laugh. "Broken air conditioner, leaky pipe under the kitchen sink, walls as thin as fucking paper."

"Welcome to the building." I swing my arms in the air.

"I'm monthly, so I'm bailing next week. Harold can't keep up with the repairs in my place, and my DIY skills are shit." He looks past my shoulder to my apartment. "I see you didn't get the view."

I glance over at Rocco. "I actually have the best view in the city."

"It's all in the eye of the beholder." Gage rubs his temple. "I came to say I'm sorry for all the noise. I'll be out of earshot soon."

"Lucky you," I joke. "It was nice to meet you."

He tilts his head, his gaze volleying back and forth between Rocco and me. "Seems as though you two are the lucky ones."

"We're the lucky ones?" I question with a cocked brow.

Wiping a hand across his forehead, he smiles. "You found each other in a sea of millions of faces. I consider that lucky, don't you?"

"We're just...I mean we are..." I stumble with what to say. We're lovers, but are we more?

"We're lucky that fate crossed our paths." Rocco steps in to save me.

"Fate," Gage repeats back with a nod of his head. "We're all at her mercy, aren't we?"

"Indeed." Rocco's hand moves to the middle of my back. "Fate calls all the shots."

Gage looks at us once more. "Enjoy your night."

"We will," Rocco says, his gaze sliding to my face. "We definitely will."

Chapter 50

Rocco

"Dexie," I hiss her name out between clenched teeth.

Looking down at my lap, that mane of pink-streaked hair is all I see. I'm sitting in a chair. My cock is buried in her mouth, sliding down her velvet throat.

"Stop." I groan the word out wrapped in a heavy exhale. "I want to come in you."

She shakes her head from side-to-side, her tongue strumming along the thick vein under the crown.

With a pop her lips are free. "You want to come in my mouth."

I do. Jesus, do I want that, but there's nothing that feels as good as her cunt squeezing me when I shoot my load.

I fist her hair in my hands to keep her mouth off of me. "No more."

Her tongue lashes out to swipe over the head, jerking my cock. "More."

I twist my hands. "I need a condom."

"Fuck me later," she mewls as she looks up at me from where she's kneeling on my bedroom floor. Her lips are swollen and pink. Her eyes hooded.

"Condom," I repeat, unfettered lust consuming me.

She leans back on her heels. "Get the condom so I can sit in your lap."

Goddamn this woman.

I push her aside and stalk toward the nightstand. I tug the drawer open and empty the box on the bed, sending condom packages flying everywhere.

"Someone's in a hurry."

I glance over at her. Her tits are bouncing as she laughs. Her hair is a mess.

I rip open a package and sheath myself. "Come sit on me."

I settle onto the bed, my back against the headboard. I close my eyes, willing the weight in my chest to fuck the hell off.

I've been torn between wanting to fuck her and tell I love her since we left her apartment.

I watched her earlier. I know what she said to me.

The word '*love*' left her lips when she stood by her window staring at me.

She crawls across the bed on her hands and knees like an alley cat out to get their prey.

Does she not know that she caught me in her snare before we ever spoke a word to each other? It's not only my dick that is aching to be inside of her. The rest of me wants in her heart, her mind, in all of her.

"Get on my cock," I demand in a low voice. "Fuck me."

"My pleasure," she purrs as she climbs over my legs and settles with her cunt grazing the head of my cock.

I want to rip the condom off so I can savor the smoothness of her. I want to feel that wet heat surround me.

"Be gentle?" she asks with a lift of both brows.

It's taking every ounce of strength within me to control the need. My hands inch toward her bare skin. I want to bite it, bruise it. I want her to feel me tomorrow and every day after.

She grabs hold of the base of my dick and I groan aloud. "Fuck me, Dexie. Just fuck me."

She lowers herself onto me, inch by deliciously dizzying inch until I'm buried to the hilt.

I let her set the pace. Achingly slow strokes of her cunt over my cock drive me mad.

I rest my head against the headboard and stare at her as she rides me.

Her eyes are closed, her lips parted enough to reveal those two overlapping teeth and her hair flows down her back as she takes what she needs from me.

"I love you," I whisper so softly that I know she can't hear.

She arches her body, her hands leaping back to rest on my thighs and she fucks me hard, chanting my name over and over, imprinting every nuance of this perfect moment into my memory.

***

"What's the cure for a sore pussy?" Dexie snuggles under the blanket on my bed.

"My tongue." I stick it out.

"No." She shakes her head. "It was so deep. I don't think I've ever come that hard before."

I know I haven't. I shook through my orgasm, holding her tightly to my chest as I pumped out every last drop.

"I take that as a challenge." I hand her a bottle of water.

She takes a sip. "A challenge?"

"I can make you come harder than that."

She gazes at my semi-erect penis. "Not tonight."

"Tonight." I take the water from her and down a gulp.

The sound of my phone ringing catches her by surprise. She jerks her head to look over at it sitting on the nightstand. "Saved by the bell."

I laugh. "You're not getting off that easy."

"I see what you did there." She closes her eyes. "You get me off easy, Rocco. Your hands, your mouth, that big beautiful cock of yours."

My phone quiets but only for a second. It starts ringing again.

"It's after midnight," she says quietly. "Answer it."

I do. I pick it up, my brow furrowing when I see who is calling. I swipe my finger over the screen to answer it. "Pop?"

His voice quivers on the other end. "I need you, son."

"I'm coming," I say without hesitation. "I'm on my way."

Chapter 51

Rocco

Four hours later I'm staring out the window.

It's not the view I wanted or expected.

I'm not looking into the apartment of the only woman I've ever loved. I'm gazing at Manhattan as it starts to wake.

It's a typical day for most of the city. People will roll over in bed to see the face they adore.

They'll eat breakfast, brush their teeth, dress and head off to wherever they earn a paycheck.

It's a day like any other for most of New York City.

It's another day in hell for my father; for me.

I glance over to where he's sitting on a chair. His eyes are closed, but he's awake. He's been up all night.

The sound of an announcement over the intercom system cracks one of his eyelids open.

"Are they..."

"No." I glance back out the window. "No word yet."

I scrub my hands over my face as I listen to him sigh. "How, Rocco? How did this happen?"

How did we end up in a hospital again waiting for news about the woman who owns his heart? How the hell do we get through the conversation with the doctor who will explain to my father why his new bride took a nap after dinner last night and didn't wake up when he tried to rouse her?

How do I hold my father up through the loss of another woman he loves?

"Let's wait for the doctor, Pops." I try to sound upbeat. I have enough fucking practice doing that.

I did it when Irena was wheeled into this same hospital three years ago on a gurney after she collapsed on a sidewalk.

She had just left my apartment ten minutes before.

Ten fucking minutes.

We had spent the morning at the Met together and then had lunch at her favorite French restaurant before we went back to my apartment for a cup of coffee.

I had hugged her, told her I loved her, and she set off to see my sister.

Some stranger called an ambulance after they watched her fall to the concrete.

She never regained consciousness. She died in this hospital as I sat in the waiting room holding tight to my father's hand.

It was the same after my mother died.

It was days short of my seventh birthday, but that fact got lost in the grief.

My dad told me endless stories about my mom in the years after she died.

He cried every day.

I tried to soothe him but what can a kid do when his own heart is broken into a million pieces? "Mr. Jones?"

We both turn at the mention of our names.

My dad pushes himself up from his chair, his knees wobbling. I go to him, wrapping my arm around his shoulder.

"April is resting."

"Is she awake?" My father asks in a strained voice that I've heard too many times in my life.

"No, sir. She's still unconscious." The doctor kneads his hands together. "We're waiting for the results of the tests. We'll know more when…"

"When you get those," I finish for him. "When will that be?"

"I put a rush on them." He looks to my father and then me. "You can sit with her if you like."

My dad looks up at me, his brown eyes sullen and cloudy with a grief that's been there more often than not in my lifetime.

This is the price you pay for love.

The words he said to me when I was eight-years-old echo in my mind.

"Did you call…"

"I called," I assure him. "Chloe is on her way. Nash is out of town, but Luke will come as soon as his shift is done."

"I'll sit with her." He nods his head slowly. "I'll sit until she wakes up."

I pray to god that happens soon.

My phone chimes in the pocket of my jeans. I slide it out.

Dexie: *I know it's late, but is everything all right? You left so quickly.*

I had left her in my bed when I hastily dressed and took off. I told her it was a family issue because that's what this is. It's an issue that my family has dealt with far too many times.

"Is that Chloe?" My dad cranes his neck to look at the screen of my phone.

"No, Pops." I kiss his forehead. "Let's go see April." He leans against me. "I promised myself I'd never love again. My heart can't do this, Rocco."

The pain he's in is palpable. I feel it in every cell of my body.

I can't do it either.

Chapter 52

Dexie

Rocco: *Everything is fine.*

I reread the text Rocco sent me three days ago. It's the last I've heard from him.

He hasn't picked up when I've called him. My texts since then have gone unanswered and his apartment has been dark since I let myself out the other morning, locking the door behind me.

I step forward when the elevator doors fly open.

"Dexie." Rhoda approaches me. "I was just about to leave."

"What are you doing here?" I look past her to where Shona is seated behind the reception desk.

I treated myself to an expensive coffee at Palla on Fifth because I needed to get out of the office and my stomach hasn't been able to handle food.

There's a weight in it. It's a sinking feeling that whatever is happening in Rocco's life is going to change mine forever.

"I came to congratulate you." She claps her hands together.

I motion for her to follow me down the hallway. I offer a Shona a weak smile as we pass her desk. "Am I right to assume you're here with an offer, Rhoda, and you think I'll be accepting it?"

She follows me into my office, waiting until I close the door behind us.

"You're joking, Dexie."

I turn to face her. She's dressed as impeccably as ever. The designer handbag on her shoulder is a new piece from a collection just released last week.

I know I shouldn't allow my personal feelings to impact my business decisions, but I'm miffed that she hasn't tested my product out. If she's as interested in my handbags as she says she is, why isn't she using one?

I pop up a brow. "Joking?"

She thins her lips. "Did you promise Suzanne you wouldn't say anything until the ink was dry on your contract?"

"Suzanne Belese?" I ask while my brain tries to play catch-up with her last question.

"Your new partner." She cocks both brows.

I shake my head. "I have no idea what you're talking about."

"Rocco told me." She slaps the top of my hand. "Technically, Rocco convinced me to back off so you'd accept Suzanne's deal. I have to admit, it's the best choice for you."

I lean a hip against the side of my desk and repeat my last words. "I have no idea what you're talking about."

She tugs on the green silk scarf around her neck. "What do you mean you have no idea what I'm talking about?"

I shrug both shoulders.

Her gaze bounces from my face to the wall behind me. "Rocco called me late last night and told me to drop my interest in your company."

He did what?

"I told him to go to hell," she goes on, "I've always viewed myself as the best partner for you. No one understands the beauty of a designer bag more than I do."

She twirls her handbag around.

"I had my offer ready to go." She moves to settle into a chair in front of my desk. "Rocco told me about what Suzanne is offering you. I can't match that."

I haven't heard a peep out of Suzanne since I had lunch with her and Rocco.

"What is she offering me?"

Rhoda crosses her legs at the knee. "Are you seriously telling me that you don't know about this?"

"I'm dead serious." I rest my head in my hands. "Please, Rhoda, tell me what the hell is going on."

"You haven't talked to Rocco or Suzanne about this?"

I look up at her. "No. I haven't."

"I let the chicken out of the coop." She pushes to stand. "It's not my place to tell you what I know."

"Please sit." I motion to the chair she just rose from. "This is my business. It's my life. Who I partner with is my decision. I have a right to know."

She tosses me a brisk nod. "You're right."

I watch in silence as she sits back down.

She runs her hands over the front of her navy blue pants. "Rocco told me that Suzanne will take you under her wing. Dexie Walsh will become a subsidiary of Belese. You'll use their manufacturer and your bags will be in the Belese boutiques right next to Suzanne's bags. You'll retain creative control. The numbers work in your favor Dexie. You trade a portion of equity for a royalty. It's a strong offer."

It sounds like a dream come true.

"Working side-by-side with Suzanne is just what you need." She manages a small smile. "The California sunshine is a bonus."

"California sunshine?" I question with a knit of my brow.

"You're moving to California." She looks at her handbag. "That's where Suzanne's studio is so you'll be learning the ropes there."

I pinch my eyes shut. Rocco wants this for me? He wants me to move across the country?

"Promise me you'll act surprised when Suzanne calls you." Rhoda's on her feet again. "I didn't mean to spill the beans and ruin anything."

"You didn't ruin a thing." I push to stand. "Will you see yourself out?"

She purses her lips together. "I still have an offer at the ready, Dexie. If anything changes and you want to stay in New York and work with me, I'm a phone call away."

"Thank you, Rhoda." I breathe out a sigh. "I'll remember that."

She walks out of my office, without a single glance back.

Once she's out of view, I pick up my phone and call Rocco.

The message I leave this time is short and sweet. "What the hell is going on?"

Chapter 53

Rocco

All the air leaves my lungs when I turn the corner and see Dexie standing in front of her building.

She's the most beautiful thing I've ever seen.

It's not the pink dress she's wearing or the way her hair is pulled back into a ponytail.

It's that face and the heart that beats inside that body.

The heart that owns me. It will always own me.

"Rocco." My name snaps from her lips when she sees me approaching her.

Something shifts in her expression once she looks me over.

I look like hell.

Why wouldn't I?

I've spent the past three days by my father's side as he's navigated a medical maze.

I've been home twice to shower and change clothes.

The short beard covering my jaw irritates the hell out of me, but shaving would take precious minutes away from my family.

"Dexie," I say her name and something inside of me cracks in half.

I bite back the rush of emotions that threaten to break free.

"Are you all right?" Her brown eyes narrow, a look of concern blankets her expression.

"I'm fine," I lie through my teeth. "How are you?"

"Confused," she admits on a sigh. "Pissed off."

At any other time, I'd use that to my advantage. An angry fuck with her would be intense. I've never seen her like this.

"What's wrong?" I ask the question even though I know it sounds ridiculous.

What's wrong? What the fuck is wrong with you, Rocco?
I chase away the annoying voice in my head with a hard swallow.

"We should talk about this in private." Her hand gestures to the door of my building. "Can we go up to your place?"

My place. It's where we made love and she fell asleep in my bathtub wrapped in my arms.

I open the door and motion for her to go first. She ascends the stairs in silence, her back rigid and her shoulders tense.

Once we reach my floor, I move in front of her to unlock my apartment door. I swing it open and she steps through before I do.

"I need to use the washroom," she announces before she takes off down the hallway. Her heels click out a frantic beat.

I use the time to suck in a deep breath.

I walk to the window and gaze at her apartment. It's where I first saw her.

The sound of my phone's chime drops my eyes down to the screen.

Luke: *I'm with dad. Take a few hours to yourself.*

To do what? Worry? Pace? Think about all life's what ifs?

I type back a response.

Rocco: *I'll be back soon. How are you holding up?*

His reply is almost instant.

Luke: *I'm ok but you know…I'm worried about Pop.*

"Rocco?"

I turn at the sound of her voice; her beautiful throaty voice.

"I passed by your bedroom." Her gaze darts back down the hallway. "Have you not been home since I was here?"

The twisted sheets and condom packages strewn all over the bed is proof that I haven't slept in there in days.

"Something came up." I don't have the strength to spew out the diagnosis and prognosis.

Her hands fist together in front of her. "Do you want to talk about it?"

I look back at her apartment. "Let's talk about you."

"About Suzanne?"

That pulls my gaze back to her. "You heard from her?"

"From Rhoda." She shrugs her shoulder. "She told me you called her about Suzanne."

"You should take Suzanne's offer."

That offer is a gift. Suzanne called me two days ago and I ignored every single one of her calls. She reached out to Jared and he filled her in on where I was. She came to the hospital, flowers in hand with an offer for Dexie in her head.

She wanted to run it by me first.

I was stunned. It's perfect for the growth of Dexie's business.

"You want me to move to California?" Her voice cracks. "You want me to go there?"

No. I want you to stay with me. I want you to marry me and have our children. I want to grow old with you and then a minute before you die, I want to take my last breath, so I don't have to go through the agonizing pain that my father has.

I can't live without her. I can't die after her.

I can't fucking think.

"I want your dreams to come true." I turn to her. "That's what I want most for you."

"You think my dreams are in California?"

"I think you have to consider what's best for you."

It's a cop-out. Every fucking word leaving my mouth is a waste of breath.

Her bottom lip trembles as she studies my face. "Why did you call Rhoda and tell her to drop her offer?"

"She couldn't offer you anything close to what Suzanne is." I scrub my hand over my face. "I didn't want you listening to her bullshit when you have a solid offer on the table."

"You haven't made your offer yet." She takes a step closer to me.

My offer is everything her heart desires. I'll lease a storefront on Fifth Avenue and set up a sewing machine in the middle of it. She can sell one handbag a year for all I care.

All I want is for her to feel fulfilled.

"Do you want me to stay in New York, Rocco?"

My phone rings, pushing her back a step.

I glance down.

Pop's name dances over the screen.

"I have to take this," I say, looking into her eyes.

She nods. "Take it."

I head for the kitchen. "I'll be right back."

The phone is to my ear by the time I round the corner. "Pop."

He sighs heavily. "April's latest test results are back. I need you here."

"I'm coming." I sigh into the phone. "I'll be back as soon as I can."

"I love you, boy."

"You too," I say quietly ending the call.

I rush back to the living room. "I'm sorry about that, Dexie. I'm sorry about everything."

My words are greeted with silence and an empty room.

She's gone.

Chapter 54

Dexie

I walk into Calvetti's and draw a deep breath.
I can do this.

I hope that what I'm about to give Marti will
bring a smile to her face.

I left Rocco's apartment two hours ago after
he took a call. I'm sure it was important. That's not
the reason I stormed out and went back to my office
at Matiz.

I wanted to scream at him for pulling the
strings of my life behind my back.

I needed him to tell me that California isn't
the place for me.

Rocco has never told me he loves me. I
haven't told him either.

Maybe it's best that I kept that to myself.

"Dexie." Marti raises her hand in the air in a
wave.

The lunch crowd has cleared and it's too early
for the dinner rush, so only a few people are seated at
tables.

I don't wave back because I'm holding a large
square white box in my hands.

I was going to bring this to her with Rocco on
her birthday, but I'm not sure if I'll see him again.

Suzanne dropped by my office at Matiz when I got back from Rocco's apartment. She made her offer. I told her I needed time.

She left with a smile and an assumption that I'll be packing my bags to head to Los Angeles soon.

I went home, boxed up Marti's purse, tied a big blue bow it and came straight here.

"This is for you." I push the box at Marti as she approaches me.

She gazes down at it. "For me?"

I nod.

"Come and sit. I'll make you the seafood linguine." She motions to a table in the corner.

I follow her in silence.

"Are you and Rocco partners yet?" She laughs. "He hasn't been in for a few days. I miss his face."

I miss his face too and the way he kisses me. I miss the promise that was there in his eyes the other night. Today it was replaced with distance.

"We won't be partnering."

That draws her brows up as she sits in a chair next to the table. "I'm sorry to hear that."

I rest the box on the table. "I'm not sure when your birthday is, but I wanted you to have this today."

"It's next month." She leans forward as I sit. "When you're my age you try to forget when your next birthday is."

I manage a small laugh. "Open it, Marti."

Anxiety knits her brow as her hands move to the large blue bow. She tugs on one end freeing it.

Her hands move to her lap. She stares at the box. "My heart is beating so hard."

I push my chair closer to her. "I hope that you'll like what's inside."

Her eyes scan my face. There are years of wisdom in her gaze and gracefulness that speaks of a degree of inner strength I can only hope to have one day.

She reaches for the box, tugging the lid off. She drops it on the table and peers inside.

Blue tissue paper is pushed aside by her hands and then she gasps. It's so loud that the people seated two tables away from us turn to look.

"Dexie," she whispers my name softly. "How did you do this?"

I watch as she reaches for one of the leather straps. She pulls the purse out of the box and sets it on the table in front of her.

Her fingers run over the old leather that's now bordered by new leather a shade darker.

The straps are new. The buckle closing the purse is as well.

I was able to save the interior. I stitched it back together with an edging of new silk.

Marti didn't need a new purse. The purse her daughter gave her needed some love and extra care.

Her hand slides along the interior to the zippered compartment. A soft smile curves her lips when she feels the card safely inside.

I know we won't speak about it. To her, I'm little more than a stranger, but to me, she's a woman I'll always remember.

She reaches across the table to take my hand in hers. "This is a gift. Thank you."

I squeeze her hand. "It was my honor to fix that up for you."

"I'll get that linguine."

I know she shows her appreciation through food. I saw it when I was here with Rocco.

"I need to go." I look into her eyes. "Thank you for trusting me with your purse."

Her gaze locks on mine. "You're an angel. Life is going to give you good things."

I'm just a woman, unsure of what tomorrow is going to bring, but certain that I'll get through it.

"I'll take a rain check on the linguine," I say even though I doubt I'll ever step foot in here again.

This is where Rocco's family gathers. I'll never be a part of that.

"Where are you off to?" She pushes to her feet.

"I hear California is nice this time of year."

"It's nice any time of the year."

I stand too. "Take care, Marti."

She takes me into an embrace, her hand patting the middle of my back. "Trust your heart. Always trust your heart."

I pull back. "Trust my heart?"

Her fingers skim over my chin. "I know a broken heart when I see one. Give it time to heal and then you trust where it takes you."

"I will," I say softly. "I promise I will."

Chapter 55

Dexie

I scan the interior of Palla on Fifth until I find the friendly face I'm looking for. I head straight to it.

"Gina," I say her name with a smile. "It's good to see you."

She jumps to her feet to wrap her arms around me. "Dexie."

I knew when she reached out and asked me to meet her that it was about Marti's purse.

She tracked me down on Instagram. She followed me. I followed her and here we are.

"Can I get you a coffee?"

I shake my head. "I've had three cups already today. I'm good."

"I'll get some water," she says before I can decline the offer.

She marches over to the counter and says something to Palla. Palla grabs a bottle of water, tosses me a wave and kisses Gina's cheek.

I glance over at the table where I sat with Rocco.

Tears bubble inside of me, but I push them back down with a heavy swallow.

I promised myself this morning that I wouldn't cry today, but I broke down five minutes after I got out of bed and looked over at Rocco's apartment.

There was no movement or sign of him.

Gina sits back down in her chair and slides the bottle of water at me. "Palla will bring us some pastries when she has a minute."

I haven't eaten anything more than a few pieces of fruit in days.

"I'm not hungry." I take a sip of the water. "How do you know Palla?"

I ask the question, so she'll talk. It's easier listening to other people tell their stories.

"Her husband Arlo is my cousin."

"He's your cousin?" I question back.

"I come here because I never have to pay for a cup of coffee." She tosses her head back in laughter. "Don't tell Rocco."

She has nothing to worry about there. Rocco and I have nothing left to say to each other.

"Every single time I've met Rocco here for coffee, he pays for it." She rolls her eyes. "Why pay for coffee when you own the place?"

I scratch the back of my head. "Rocco owns this place?"

"With Arlo and Palla." She runs her finger along the rim of the coffee mug in front of her. "This is Arlo's dream. Rocco made it happen. It's what he does."

He's a good man with a kind heart; a kind heart that will never belong to me.

I take a sip of the water to avoid having to reply to that. What can I say about Rocco that won't leave me crying?

I love him. I want him to love me back.

That's not the reality I'm living in.

"I asked you to meet me to thank you for what you did for my grandma." She bites her bottom lip. "She showed me the purse a few days ago, Dexie. I can't remember the last time I saw her that happy."

A smile blooms on my lips. "Your grandma is a really special person."

"So are you." Her eyes skim my face. "You put a lot of thought and care into that bag. I don't think anyone else would have done that."

Maybe. Maybe not.

I had to because I knew that to Marti it was priceless.

My phone chimes in my purse luring Gina's eyes to it. I open the baby blue satchel and tug out my phone. It's a text from Shona. It's nothing urgent, so I drop my phone back in and clasp it shut.

"Did you make that?" Gina circles her finger in front of the purse.

I nod. "I did."

"Dexie, that's gorgeous."

I like that she thinks so. She's dressed in a low cut dress today that's the same shade of red as the blouse and pants I'm wearing. The heels on her feet are a designer brand. She looks like she just stepped off a runway.

Her fashion sense is killer.

"Thank you." I smile at the compliment. "I'm glad you like it."

"Can I buy it?" She laughs. "Or one like it?"

"You want to buy one of my bags?"

"Or more," she says tentatively. "Do you have a website? Is there a place where I can see what you have available?"

"My apartment." I glance at the watch on my wrist. "I have a bit of time after work. We can meet there."

She rubs her chin. "When are you done work?"

"An hour and a half from now."

I've been staying late every night to avoid the windows in my apartment and the off chance that I might see Rocco. I need to leave my office at quitting time today. There's somewhere I need to be at nine o'clock tonight.

"I'll wait here." She leans back in her chair. "Swing by and pick me up when you're done for the day so I can go purse shopping."

Chapter 56

Rocco

"It's not a good time, Gina," I say into my phone. "I've got a lot going on."

"Like what?" she spits back.

"I can't get into it now." I point my hand toward the corner, directing my attention to the taxi driver. "Turn right up there. It's faster."

I lean back against the worn leather seat.

"Are you on your way home?" She questions, the sounds of the city behind her.

"Why?" I push back. "Who broke your heart today?"

"Meet me at the restaurant."

"I can't." I curse under my breath when we slow in heavy traffic.

I'm on my way to my apartment, so I can shower, check in with Jared about a few pressing issues, and then round up some food to take back to the hospital.

"Meet me now," she insists. "This is important."

"Fine, Gina. I'm a block from there. I'll see you soon." Ending the call, I pull my wallet out of the pocket of my jeans and toss the driver a few bills. "Keep the change."

Opening the car door, I slide out and weave my way through the traffic to the sidewalk.

I spot Gina as she rounds the corner with at least a half dozen brightly colored handbags in her hands.

I stalk toward her reaching out my hands to take some of the bags from her. I recognize them.

Dexie's hands have touched them. Her careful attention has gone into every detail of the design of these handbags.

"Thank you," Gina says breathlessly. "I went to your place, but obviously you weren't there."

I haven't told Gina about April yet. She loves my Pop. They may not be related by blood, but their bond is strong.

I'll have to hold Gina's hand through this too and I can't do that until I know exactly what we're facing.

I called in a specialist this morning. Once she's had a look at April, I can sit down with the family and share the news.

"I'm busy, Gina." I know I sound brusque, but I'm running on two hours a sleep a night and coffee.

"You need to see what Dexie did for grandma."

I don't need to see that. A thread is holding my heart together. It's tenuous.

We stand at the light waiting to cross. "What did she do?"

I'd rather hear about it than see it. Once I walk into Calvetti's Marti will take one look at me and know my world is falling apart around me.

"You'll see," she says before starting across the street.

I follow one step behind her until we reach the door to my grandmother's restaurant.

Gina pulls it open and walks in. I follow wishing to fuck that I wouldn't have answered that call.

***

"It's beautiful, Rocco." Marti swings her purse in the air in a circle. "Just look at what she did for me."

I can't look at it anymore.

It's too much.

All of this is too fucking much for me.

"I bought all of these from her today." Gina glances over at the array of handbags she placed on the table next to us.

"I already posted one to my Instagram." She waves her phone in my direction. "Over twenty thousand likes already. Dexie's business is about to blow up."

"You saw her today?"

Both Marti and Gina look over at me. I heard my voice. It doesn't sound like me.

Gina's oblivious to the pain in it. "I was with her right before I came here."

I clear my throat. "How is she?"

Marti turns in her seat to look right at me, but she doesn't say a word.

"She seems sad." Gina shrugs. "I don't know Dexie very well, but she seemed sad."

"Gina, get me a glass of red wine." Marti's arm flies in the air. "Take your time."

Gina's eyes are glued to her phone. "In a minute. My post about Dexie's purse is blowing up."

"Go." Marti looks over at her. "Now."

"Fine." Gina pushes to her feet. "I'm grabbing one for myself too."

Marti waits until Gina is out of earshot. "That's not a surprise."

I smile faintly. "How are you, Marti?"

"Mad at you."

I toss my head back on a sigh. "I'm sorry I haven't been in. There's a lot of shit going on right now."

"Your mother wouldn't like that language."

I don't need the reminder about my mother, or Irena, or April, or Dexie for that matter.

"This is why Dexie has a broken heart." She pushes on my elbow. "You broke that girl's heart. I saw the pain in her face the other day."

Digging the palms of my hands into my eye sockets, I shake my head. "We're not doing this, Marti. I can't do this."

She tugs on my forearm. "You love her."

"With everything I am," I admit as tears fill my eyes.

"She loves you."

I wipe my hands over my cheeks. "It doesn't matter."

"Like hell, it doesn't." Her hand leaps to cover her mouth. "You've never loved a woman before."

I take a deep breath before I blow out a long exhale. "I can't, Marti."

"Can't what?" She squeezes my shoulder. "Tell me what you can't do."

"Marry her, watch her have my children, build a life with her and then wake up one morning without her."

Tears stream down her cheeks. "Can you wake up every morning now without her?"

No. I can't go to sleep without her. I can't fucking breathe without her.

I turn my head to look at her, wiping a tear from her cheek. "What happens if I lose her one day?"

"You don't worry about that day." She holds my hand to her cheek. "You worry about all the days you have with her. Each one of those days is a gift."

I scrub my hand over the back of my neck.

"Loss is part of life." Her mouth softens into a smile. "If someone would have told me that your grandfather wouldn't be here with me now, I still would have married him."

"You would have?"

"Over and over again." She squeezes my hand. "I wouldn't have traded one day with him for a lifetime with another man."

"I need to go." I kiss her hand. "I'll be back when I can."

"You go to her." She looks into my eyes. "You tell her that you love her and you never let that girl go."

Chapter 57

Dexie

My phone chimes again inside my black leather tote.

My Instagram follower count has been ballooning since Gina left my apartment. I watched her post a picture of one of my handbags with a tag to my account. She has millions of followers, which means a lot of potential customers.

I glance out the window of the Uber as we maneuver through the early evening traffic of Manhattan.

"What time is your flight?" The driver has been trying to chitchat me up since he picked me up.

I've kept my answers short and sweet. I'll do the same now.

I glance down at the watch on my wrist. "I have time."

He nods as he gazes at me in the rearview mirror. I'm not a sight to behold.

After Gina left my apartment, I finished packing my overnight bag and then I changed into jeans, a blue T-shirt and sneakers.

My phone chimes again so I dig it out of my bag.

I manage a smile when I read the text message on the screen.

Sophia: *I hate you.*

I type out an instant response.

Dexie: *You love me.*

I watch as the three dots bounce on the screen as she replies.

Sophia: *Who will wear my clothes if you move to California?*

Dexie: *People wear clothes there.*

Sophia: *Text me when you land?*

Dexie: *I will. I'm turning off my phone now to conserve the battery. I forgot my charger.*

Sophia: *They have chargers there, but not a best friend like me. I'm just saying.*

I laugh inwardly as I slide the phone to its off position, toss it back in my purse and close my eyes.

***

I thought I'd spend my day in Los Angeles with Suzanne, but I've been delegated to one of her assistants.

I can't complain. Suzanne is funding this trip so I can get a better sense of how Belese works and where I fit into their big picture.

I brush my hair back from my face.

So far this trip has confirmed what my heart had been telling me since Suzanne made her offer.

I belong in New York City.

"As you can see the boutique is divine." Marla, the redheaded assistant, twirls in a circle in the middle of the small store that is home to Belese in L.A.

"It's lovely."

"Suzanne's vision is a corner over there for Dexie Walsh." She motions to where a purple velvet chair is. "I'll be working hand-in-hand with you to get your collection set up."

I sold most of my collection to Gina yesterday afternoon.

My phone beeps again. It's been non-stop as notification after notification sounds.

I woke up in the uncomfortable hotel bed to dozens of missed calls, more than a hundred emails, five hundred text messages, and tens of thousands of new Instagram followers.

Gina has done more for my business with one social media post than I've been able to do in years of trying.

Another text message comes in from a New York based number.

I removed my phone number from my website before I left the hotel this morning, but a few messages are still landing on my phone.

I only read a handful before I gave up.

I already have enough potential handbag orders to keep me busy for the next two years.

"You seem preoccupied." Marla juts her hip out. "Should we do this later? Is tomorrow better for you?"

"I'm going back to New York tomorrow morning," I point out. "I'll silence the phone."

She gives me the once-over again. I'm still wearing the same white maxi-dress and red flats that I put on this morning.

I could tell from her expression when I arrived at the boutique that she didn't approve. I didn't care.

I drop my phone back in my purse.

"Suzanne is thinking five bags a season to start." She claps her hands together in mock glee. "Do you want to head over to the design studio?"

I want to absorb every ounce of information I can about how Suzanne Belese runs her business because when I get back to Manhattan, I plan on finding an investor who will fund my replication of it.

Chapter 58

Rocco

"Your mother used to bring you here," my dad says as he gazes up at a tree, the branches whipping in the light wind, sending a leaf floating down. "It was in the afternoon after lunch at Calvetti's."

My memories of those days are spot-on. I can draw up an image of Nash in a stroller and my pregnant mom walking along one of the paths here in Bryant Park.

After her death, my dad kept the tradition up, bringing us down here every week.

He'd sit on a bench and weep. My brothers and I would kick around a soccer ball and then we'd go home and have dinner.

"It's just us four men now," my dad would comment before we'd fall asleep.

"How's April?" I rest a hand on his shoulder.

We're stopped in the middle of the park. I dragged him out of the hospital to shower and change his clothes. It was his idea to take a walk here.

I needed the fresh air too. I've been trying to reach Dexie since I left Calvetti's last night. I haven't heard a word back.

"It's going to take time, Rocco." He bows his head. "Time for us to adjust."

Adjust to a diagnosis that will ultimately leave him a widower again.

A tumor is sitting at the base of April's brain. It's inoperable. She has time. No one can guarantee how much, but treatment will give her more days with my dad.

Chloe's husband, Evan, is a doctor. He's been helping my dad and April understand it all.

"I'm sorry, Pop." It's the first time I've said it since he was given the news.

He turns to look at me. "I talked to Marti this morning."

It's always been my job to deliver bad news to the family.

I was the one who called everyone to gather at Marti's restaurant after Irena passed. I broke down when I told them that my mother had died.

Irena was my mother as much as Gaia was.

April is a friend. I'll do whatever I can for her.

My money affords the luxury of the best medical care.

"She told me about Dexie." A half smile tugs at his mouth. "Her name is Dexie, right?"

"Dexie," I repeat back.

"You haven't brought her around." He looks up at the blue sky again. "I want to meet her."

I can't promise him that will happen. I don't know what Dexie feels, or what her future holds.

I'll pack up my life tomorrow and follow her to California if she'll grant me that privilege, but she's not answering any of my calls or text messages, so my suitcase is still in the hall closet, and my heart is on hold.

"I need to say something to you." Looking up at me, my dad shields his eyes from the morning sun. "Listen. Don't interrupt."

I dig my hands into the pockets of my jeans. "Go for it, Pop."

"You are the son." He pats the center of my chest with his hand. "I am the dad."

I bite my lip to avoid a terse remark about that obvious fact.

"It was my job to help you grieve." His voice quakes. "I gave you that job and I shouldn't have."

I shake my head. "Pop, I..."

"No interruptions." He reaches up to grab my shoulders. "I put too much on you. These shoulders are strong, but mine are too."

I nod.

"Don't be afraid to love this woman, Rocco." A smile spreads on his face. "A father's joy in his children's happiness."

"You'll bring her to meet me," he goes on, "I'll love her too and you'll never take one day with her for granted."

"I won't," I respond quietly. "I'll cherish every single one of them."

"We're going to be all right." He pats his palm against my cheek. "You go and be happy. That's what I want."

It's what I want too. I hope to hell it's what Dexie wants.

***

Dread seeps into my belly as I stare out the windows of my apartment.

I can't see into Dexie's place anymore.

Sometime between my stop here last night and now, Harold must have installed blinds over the three windows that used to give me a clear view into the life of the woman I adore.

I tug my phone out of my pocket and try and call her again.

It goes straight to voicemail with a warning that her mailbox is full.

I can't even fucking leave her a message.

I scroll through the logged calls on my phone and pull up a number I have no right calling.

I press the number to dial it.

"Hello."

"This is Rocco Jones. I apologize for calling you out of the blue like this, but we need to talk."

Chapter 59

Dexie

I turn my phone on once the plane lands at La Guardia.

The chirp of notifications is endless, so I silence it while I scan the screen.

The last text message to pop up is from Sophia.

My heart stops as I read it once and then again.

Sophia: *I'm at Lennox Hill Hospital Emergency. Please come as soon as you land.*

I ignore the flight attendant's warning not to use any phones until we're settled at the gate.

As the airplane taxis on the runway, I call Sophia's number.

Nothing.

I try again and it shoots straight to voicemail a second time.

I type out a message to her.

Dexie: *What's wrong? Is it Winter? Did something happen to her?*

I undo my seat belt even though we're at least two hundred feet from the gate.

One of the flight attendants waves her finger at me from where she's sitting, buckled into her seat.

First class, courtesy of Belese, is lovely but it puts me in direct eye view of the flight staff.

The woman leans forward, her voice barely more than a whisper. "You need to buckle back up."

"My best friend is at the hospital," I whisper back, my voice shaking. "I can't get in touch with her."

She taps her hand in the air. "We'll get you on your way as soon as possible."

It's not going to be soon enough.

I type out a message to Nicholas, Sophia's husband.

Dexie: *Is Sophia all right? Is Winter okay?*

The battery light in the upper corner of my phone flashes before the screen goes dark.

***

I rush through the doors of the hospital. I have my overnight bag slung over one shoulder, my black tote over the other.

I'm racing faster than my sneakers can keep up with.

I almost trip as I round the corner to the waiting room.

I spot Nicholas immediately. He's standing near the admittance desk.

I rush over to him.

"Nicholas." His name comes out in a broken voice; my broken voice. "Who is it? Tell me everyone is all right."

"Dexie." He pulls me into his chest, his strong arms wrapping around me. "I got your text. You didn't get mine?"

I step back and look up at his face. "My phone battery died."

"Ah." He nods, pushing his glasses up the bridge of his nose. "We're good. We are all good."

I bend over from the rush of relief I feel. "Is it Sophia?"

"She fainted." He leans his hand on my shoulder. "She was having coffee with your friend. He literally caught her and brought her in."

"With my friend?"

"Rocco Jones," he answers casually as if it's the norm for Sophia to have coffee with the man I love.

"Why were they having coffee together?" I run a hand over my forehead to push my hair back.

He shrugs a shoulder. "He called her when we were eating brunch. She took off after that to meet him."

I glance around the waiting room, hoping to catch a glimpse of Rocco.

"Sophia's in exam room five." He gestures down a corridor. "She'll want to see you."

I drop my bags at his feet.

He picks them up and slings them over his shoulder. "I've got these. Go."

I take off down the corridor, smoothing my hand over my T-shirt. I march into the exam room to see my best friend tucking a white blouse into a pair of red shorts.

"You're okay?" I rush to her.

She takes me into her arms. "I'm good, Dexie. I'm so good."

Something breaks inside of me and I sob in her arms. "I was so scared when I got your text."

"The nurse told me to shut off my phone when I got here." She points at her phone on the gurney. "I'm sorry I didn't have a chance to clarify what was going on."

"What is going on?" Wiping tears from my face, I take a step back and look her over.

Her hands land on her stomach. "I'm pregnant."

"You're pregnant?" My mouth drops open.

I knew they were trying, but it's been months since she's talked about having another baby. I didn't pry because I knew that if there were news, I'd be one of the first to find out.

"I was at Palla on Fifth with Rocco. He called me because he's been trying to reach you." She fans herself. "That man is a dreamboat, Dexie. He is so crazy about you."

I stand in stunned silence, unsure what to say to that.

"He loves you," she goes on, "I'm telling you he is so in love with you."

"He loves me?"

"Enough to move to California with you. He told me that he wants to." She tilts her head. "I think you should stay here and be the godmother to this baby."

"You want me to be the baby's godmother?" I look down at her flat stomach. I know it's early, but the prospect of watching Sophia go through another pregnancy is exciting.

"I want you to have everything you want."

"I want Rocco," I say without thinking.

"Go get him." She points at the corridor.

I do. I set off to find the man I can't live without.

Chapter 60

Rocco

I step out of the shower and wrap a towel around my waist.

I took the time to shave before I got under the hot water. I needed it.

My morning was spent at Lennox Hill Emergency with Sophia and her husband, Nick.

He's as good of a guy as his brother, Liam.

I was glad I was there to help when Sophia lost her balance at Palla's.

She fainted briefly, so I got Palla to flag down a taxi and I took her to the hospital.

On the way there she told me that Dexie belongs with me.

I told her she was damn right.

After a visit with my Pop and April, I dropped in to see Marti.

She fed me, asked me if I had put a ring on Dexie's finger yet and laughed when I told her to slow the hell down.

I've thought about it more in the past twenty-four hours than I care to admit.

Marriage has never been part of my plan, now it's all I want.

It's fast. It's soon, but that pink-haired beauty owns my heart.

My only job now is convincing her of that.

I walk out into the living room as dusk cloaks the city. I fell into bed after I got home from seeing Marti. Sleep came easily although it only lasted a couple of hours.

My heart stops for a full beat when I gaze out the window toward Dexie's apartment.

The blinds are up, the overhead lights are on and she's sitting on the windowsill dressed in a pair of jeans and a pink T-shirt.

It's exactly what she was wearing the first night she saw me.

I rest my forehead against my window. "Look at me, my love."

Her head turns slowly in my direction, a smile blooming on her lips.

"I love you," I say as loud as I can.

She looks down at her phone.

Mine chimes in the bedroom. I ignore it.

She raises hers in the air and waves it at me.

I turn on my heel and race to get mine.

I read the text message she just sent.

Dexie: *What did you say? I didn't quite get that. Say it again.*

I don't text her back. I dial her number as I stalk back into the living room.

She glances at her phone when it starts ringing.

"Rocco."

Jesus, I will never tire of hearing my name come from her lips.

"I love you," I say the words I've been longing to say for weeks.

Her hand leaps to the window. "I love you too."

I press my hand to my window. "I'm moving to California with you."

"I'm staying in New York with you," she sounds back.

"You are?"

She nods. "You're here. My life is here. I'm not going anywhere."

"You're wrong about that."

The corners of her lips dip into a frown. "I'm wrong about what?"

I laugh. "You're coming over here, unless…"

"Come here." She curls a finger at me. "I have blinds now."

I turn my back to her and drop the towel.

"Holy shit!" she screams into the phone. "Turn around."

I start to, but her voice stops me in place. "No, don't. I don't want anyone else seeing that. You're all mine."

"Get undressed." I hurry toward my bedroom to pull on a pair of sweatpants. "I am three minutes away from devouring you."

***

She swings her apartment door open to jump into my arms.

I catch her easily as she wraps her legs around my waist.

"I know." She rains kisses on my cheeks. "I went to Calvetti's this afternoon. I was trying to find you. Marti told me you had just left to go home to sleep. She told me everything. I know about your mom, and Irena and April."

It was my story to tell her, but I'm damn glad Marti saw her way into the middle of this.

"I'm sorry, Rocco." She rests her forehead against mine as I push her apartment door closed with a shove of my foot.

"The day you came to my place, so much was happening." I heave a sigh. "I was scared, Dexie."

"I'm here for you." She slides down my body to her feet. "I will always be here for you."

"That works both ways." I cradle her face in my hands. "You need anything, I'm right here."

Her hands crawl down my stomach to the waistband of my sweatpants. "I need to make love with you."

I glance behind her at the windows. The blinds are down, the city shut off from our small world.

I drag her T-shirt over her head to reveal her perfect breasts.

"I'm learning how to love." I lean down and take her nipple in my mouth. "Bear with me while I figure it all out."

Her hand dives into my sweatpants to circle my aching cock. "I'm learning how to love too."

I don't have to question her. Whatever she felt for anyone else doesn't compare to this. The look in her eyes tells me that.

"Come to bed with me." She tugs on my hand and takes a step back.

I follow her because this is my destiny. This woman is my every tomorrow.

Chapter 61

Dexie

"It's nice to meet you." I clear my throat. "It's so nice to meet you, Mr. Jones."

"What the hell is going on in there?" Rocco calls from my bed.

I laugh as I swipe mascara over my eyelashes. "I'm putting on my makeup."

"You're talking about me," he yells back.

"Your dad," I correct him as I take one last look at myself in the bathroom mirror.

It'll have to do.

I've been awake for two hours. I showered, dried my hair, straightened it, and tried on three different outfits before Rocco woke up.

I finally decided on a simple blue dress Sophia designed last year.

"My dad will want you to call him Pop." Rocco rounds the corner to lean against the doorjamb of the bathroom.

He's nude.

It catches my breath in my throat.

"Pop," I repeat back.

"You're going to be his daughter-in-law soon so fall into that habit now."

"Rocco," I whisper, tears threatening to ruin my mascara.

"Don't tell me that you don't want to marry this." He throws his hands in the air. "You do."

I nod. "Yes."

"This is not a proposal." He moves closer to me. "It's a promise that when things settle, I'll be dropping to one knee so I can slide my mother's engagement ring on that finger."

I look down at my left hand. "My head is spinning."

"I've waited for thirty-five-years to find you." He tugs me against his body. "I'm not wasting another day."

I look up into his handsome face. "I don't want to waste time either."

He slaps his hand on my ass. "I'm going home to get showered and changed and then we'll go see Pop."

I suck in a deep breath. "I can't wait to meet him."

***

"I'm not Mr. Jones. I'm Pop."

"Pop," I say his name. "I'll call you Pop."

Rocco's dad cradles my hand in his. We're at his home in Queens. His wife, April, is resting in the next room.

Luke was here when we arrived. I was greeted with a warm hug and a kiss on the cheek.

Rocco playfully pushed him off of me.

"Chloe and her husband want to meet you." Pop looks over to where Rocco is sitting in a chair. "Nash too."

"We'll bring dinner over one night." Rocco leans forward. "I'll cook something and if April is feeling up to it, we'll have a Jones family dinner."

"There's no better medicine than that." Pop glances back at the closed bedroom door. "She's doing better today. Her energy levels are up. I think we turned a corner."

Rocco filled me in on all the details about April's condition as we rode the subway here.

The specialist he brought in suggested a treatment plan that April is anxious to start.

"If there's anything I can do," I pause to take in a deep breath. "If I can help you or April with anything, big or small, you'll let me know?"

"You can take care of my boy." He motions to Rocco.

"I plan on doing that every day for the rest of my life."

His brown eyes well with tears. "I'm going to check on my bride."

I watch him walk away before I look back over at Rocco.

"Should we go?"

"You lead the way." He slides to his feet, his hand reaching out to me.

I take it as I stand. "I want to meet with someone. Will you come with me?"

"I'll follow you anywhere." He starts toward the door of Pop's house. "Subway or Uber?"

I skip my fingers over the screen of my phone. "An Uber. One is on its way."

"Let's sit on the porch." He swings open the door and motions for me to walk outside.

I watch as he uses a key on his key fob to lock the door behind us.

He waits for me to sit on the porch swing before he takes a seat next to me.

Taking my hand in his, he turns to face me. "Twenty-four hours ago I thought I'd blown my chance with you."

I smile softly, taking in how handsome he looks dressed in a gray lightweight sweater and jeans. I'll never get over how beautiful he is.

"I should have known something serious was going on." I glance back at the door to Pop's house. "You were so lost when I came over to your apartment that day. It was the day I thought you wanted me to move to California."

"I wanted your dreams to come true."

"They are." I lean into him. "I'm with you."

He kisses me softly on the mouth. "It's where you belong."

I glance down the street. "We're on our way to make another of my dreams come true."

"Are we?" He laughs.

"We are." I wiggle my brows. "Here comes our car."

Epilogue

One Year Later

Rocco

"Here's to my fiancée." I raise a glass of champagne in the air. "It was a year ago today that she brought me here and now look at this place."

The crowd gathered lifts their glasses in the air as Dexie beams.

Her hair is longer now, there are more pink streaks and Gaia's engagement ring is planted firmly on her finger.

We'll marry next spring after her fall collection has launched.

Today, we're celebrating the upcoming winter collection in the Dexie Walsh boutique in Soho. It's tucked next to a jewelry boutique, Whispers of Grace.

That's owned by my fiancée's business partners, Ivy Marlow-Walker, and her husband, Jax Walker.

It was Ivy who reached out to Dexie after seeing Gina's post on Instagram a year ago.

Something in Ivy's message spoke to Dexie's heart so we came down to meet her at her boutique.

That meeting turned into dinner a week later that included Jax. We hit it off immediately and I saw something in the Walkers that I admire.

They're down-to-earth people who have as much faith in Dexie and what she's doing as I am.

They offered her a deal that beat out Suzanne's.

I made an offer too, but Dexie wanted to build her company's future on her own terms. I respect every decision she makes.

Dexie and her lawyer negotiated with Ivy and Jax to secure a royalty against a small percentage of equity.

Ivy's handmade jewelry empire started in her apartment.

She worked hard for her success, and she's by Dexie's side as she does the same.

They share a studio space above Ivy's boutique. So far, Dexie has hired two women to help her craft the handbags. She'll scale up in time, at a pace that works for her.

She moved in with me a month before she quit her job at Matiz to work full-time on her business.

She's as much a part of my family as I am. Poker nights now include her. She's taken Dylan's money on more than one occasion. Nicholas's too.

Nicholas and Sophia drop by for dinner at least once a week with Winter and their new baby daughter, Reese. They've become my close friends as much as they are Dexie's.

"She's here!" Dexie starts toward the door of the boutique. My eyes are stuck on her ass in the tight pink dress she's wearing. "Rocco, come see."

I follow her smiling at people as I pass them by.

It's only invited guests tonight including Sophia and Nicholas, Dexie's mom and sister, my brothers, my sister and her husband, most of my cousins, and my dad and April.

She's still in treatment. Some days are good, others are worse, but she gets through each one with a smile as she clings to hope. We all do.

I spot Gina first as she walks through the door dressed as if she's about to hit a Paris runway. Her red dress is stunning as is the smile on her face.

"I present to you," Gina says as she waves her hand at the entrance. "Marti Calvetti."

Marti walks in wearing a simple blue dress with the purse she's carried for years slung over her shoulder. That's not what catches my eye or the eyes of everyone else in the boutique.

"I love it," Dexie whispers as she wraps her hands around my bicep. "Just look at her, Rocco."

I do.

The ear-to-ear grin on my grandmother's face is beautiful. She walks over to us and reaches out one hand to Dexie and the other to me.

We take her hands at the same time.

"What do you think, Rocco?" Her eyebrows inch up." Do you love it as much as I do?"

"I love it." I lean down to kiss her cheek. "I love you."

I never thought I'd see the day when my grandmother would walk into a room with blue streaks in her hair.

But then again, I never thought that I'd be marrying a beautiful woman with pink-streaked hair, a nose piercing and a tattoo on her wrist of the date she first saw me out her window.

I reach down to grab Dexie's left hand to plant a kiss firmly over that tattoo.

This woman has changed my life in immeasurable ways and brought a light to my family that we didn't know we needed.

She looks up and into my eyes. "I'll meet you at the window at midnight, Rocco."

"I'll be there." I smile down at her. "You can bet on that."

***

"Do you think she's happy?" Dexie calls over her shoulder as I walk into our living room ten minutes before midnight.

I peer at the dark-haired woman living in her old apartment. Two of the blinds are closed; one is still open giving us a bird's eye view into her life.

I wrap my arms around my fiancée from behind, tugging her into my bare chest. I traded the black suit I was wearing earlier for a pair of sweatpants. She's dressed in black panties and a pink tank top.

"I know I'm happy." I inhale her sweet scent. "I know five minutes from now when I'm between your legs, I'll be happier."

She reaches up to close the curtains.

When she turns to face me, I cup her cheeks in my hands. Brushing my lips against hers, I groan when I hear the moan that escapes her.

"Marry me tomorrow," I say the same three words I say to her every night.

"Maybe the day after tomorrow," she replies the same way she always does, but then she hesitates and goes on, "or maybe two months from now on a Saturday afternoon in Bryant Park."

I pull back to stare into her brown eyes. "Are we setting a date?"

"We're setting a date."

I scoop her up into my arms like the bride she'll be in just eight weeks. "We need to celebrate."

I stalk toward our bedroom.

"How will we do that?" She peppers kisses on my cheek.

"I'm about to show you," I say as I toss her on the bed.

"Will you show me every day for the rest of my life?" she asks as she watches me slide out of my sweatpants.

Groaning, I crawl over her, stopping to kiss the inside of her thigh before I move up to brush my lips over hers. "Every single day. You've made me the happiest man alive."

"I'll love you forever, Rocco," she whispers the words against my mouth.

I know she will and I'll love her for just as long.

This is our forever and we're just getting started.

Preview of Compass

A Second Chance Romance Novel

Gage Burke was supposed to be my happily-ever-after.

When he dropped to one knee on my twenty-first birthday, I saw the promise of forever in his soulful green eyes.

I picked the venue, bought the perfect wedding dress, and chose my favorite flowers for the bouquet.

Every detail was arranged, but days before the ceremony, my fiancé set sail on a new adventure without me.

I picked up the pieces of my shattered heart and patched it back together.

I left sunny California and headed east, unaware that Gage felt the same pull to New York City that I did.

When he walks into the bridal boutique I own, time stops.

He tells me that I'm his true north and that fate crossed our paths again.

I tell him to go to hell and to take fate with him.

I can't forget what happened between us in the past, even if Gage is determined to chart a new course toward our future together.

Author's note: Although a few characters from my past books make appearances in compass, it's not necessary to read any of my other books to enjoy this breathtaking romance!

Chapter 1

Kate

"I want something that is sleek and fitted, maybe a mermaid style gown, Kate."

That's not what she wants. Corly Brunton has come to my bridal shop every week for the past month to try on dresses. Three weeks ago it was mermaid style and those were all thumbs down from the group of four bridesmaids she brought with her.

Two weeks ago she was certain that she wanted a princess ball gown. Last week, she went through an off-white, off-the-shoulder phase.

"I think Natalie has the perfect dress in mind for you," I say, laughing inwardly because I know my assistant, Natalie, is going to be pissed that I'm dragging her into this.

"I love Natalie," Corly slaps her hands together. "I'm ready whenever she is."

I slip out of the change room and set out to find Natalie.

Katie Rose Bridal is busier than normal today. I attribute that to the fact that a member of the royal family tied the knot just a few days ago.

Whenever a high profile wedding takes over the headlines, business picks up.

"Natalie," I call out to her when I see her red hair peek out from behind a rack of new arrivals in the stock room.

Most of our inventory consists of vintage gowns. Natalie is standing next to a dozen dresses that just came back from the dry cleaners.

"What do you need, Kate?" Her hands drop to the waist of her simple black dress.

Everyone who works here, but me, is required to dress in black. What fun is there if the boss can't break a rule or two?

"I need you to grab that dress that came in yesterday that you thought would be perfect for Corly Brunton."

"The lace one with the beading down the bodice?" Natalie rests her hand on the rack. "Is she back?"

"She's in change room four and you're about to sell her that dress." I tug on the belt of my red dress. "I thought you'd appreciate the commission on the sale."

She narrows her green eyes. "I see right through you, Kate Wesley. As much as I would love to help Corly not find the perfect dress again, I'm busy with a bride of my own."

"I can take over that."

She scratches her chin. "This bride's budget is more than Corly's. I'm talking way more, Kate."

"The commission on both is yours, even if I make the sale."

"I'm game." She starts walking toward a rack of lace dresses. "I'll grab the dress for Corly and you'll go help Annalise Brookings find her perfect gown."

"She's in the main showroom?"

Natalie nods. "With her entourage of seven. Her fiancé and his best man are on the way too."

When I first started working in bridal I was surprised whenever a future groom showed up to witness his soon-to-be wife trying on dresses. It's not that uncommon. We have at least a few men in the showroom every week.

"What's Annalise looking for in a gown?"

"I don't have a clue." Natalie laughs as she pulls a gown in a clear garment bag from a rack. "We haven't gotten that far yet. I came back here to get a new notepad so I could jot down what she likes."

"I'm about to find out." I smile as I turn toward the showroom. "Wish me luck."

I take quick steps down the carpeted corridor that leads to the main showroom of Katie Rose Bridal.

I had it decorated in elegant and sophisticated tones. The benches are covered in cream-colored fabrics. The walls are painted pale peach. It's the perfect space to choose a dress to wear on the most important day of your life.

A bride walking back toward the change rooms catches my eye. I stare down at the gown she's trying on. It has a sweetheart neckline and a lace train. It's a beautiful dress that has brought a tear to her eye.

This is exactly why I opened this boutique.

I round the corner to the showroom and spot Annalise immediately.

She's standing near a mirror with a group of women around her. The tiara on her head is a clear sign that she's the bride.

I smile as I near her. "You must be Annalise."

"That's me." She shakes with excitement. "I'm here to find a dress."

"I'm Kate." I reach out to take her hand in mine. "I'm excited to help you do just that."

"You have perfect timing, Kate." Her hand flies in the air next to my shoulder. "My man is here with his best man."

I turn to face the double glass doors that open onto the sidewalk in front of the boutique.

Time stops.

My breathing stalls.

I stare at the two men in suits walking toward us.

One is blond with a beard and a blank look on his face as he takes in the dresses, veils and vases of flowers that decorate the space.

The other man is the one I can't take my eyes off of.

His hair is dark, his eyes a shade of green I'll never forget and the smile on his face could still light the night sky.

He slows as he nears me, his hand reaching up to touch his chest.

"Katie?" His voice rumbles through me as deeply as it did the first time I heard it.

I nod, my head moving as slow as time did when he left me days before our wedding with little explanation and a broken heart.

"Gage," I say his name softly. "Gage Burke."

Coming Soon

Preview of VERSUS

A Standalone Novel

I chose the woman I brought home with me last night for one reason and one reason only.

She looks like *her*.

It's the same with every woman I bring home with me.

They always look like *her*.

Light brown hair, sky blue eyes and a body that takes me to that place I crave. It's where I forget – *her* innocence, my cruelty, everything.

Last night was different.

This one didn't only look like *her*, she danced like *her*, spoke in a soft voice like *her,* and when she lost control on my sheets in that split second I live for, she made a sound that cracked my heart open. My heart; cold and jaded as it is, it felt a beat of something for this one.

She left before I woke up.

I need to forget about the woman from last night, just like I've forgotten every woman but the one who started me on this path to self-destruction.

I might have been able to if I wasn't standing in a crowded courtroom ready to take on the most important case of my career staring at the woman who crawled out of my arms just hours ago and into the role of opposing counsel.

I may be a high-profile lawyer, but her name is one I'd recognize anywhere.

The woman I screwed last night is the same one I screwed over in high school.

Court is now in session, and it's me versus *her*.

Chapter 1

Dylan

The world within Manhattan is its own beast. You learn that when you live here. When you claw your way around this city looking for something that's elusive.

For some, that's a job that will actually keep a roof over their heads.

For others, it's a relationship that will stand the test of time and weather the winds of change.

I have the first and no interest in the second.

My needle in the haystack is a particular type of woman.

I don't bother with blondes.

My cock has zero interest in redheads.

For me, it's all about the type of woman I see in front of me now.

Petite, light brown hair, blue eyes and a body that can move to the beat of the music.

Experience has taught me that if a woman can dance, she can fuck.

The woman I'm watching now is graceful, beautiful and within the hour will be in my bed.

I slide off the bar stool and approach her.

"I'm Dylan."

She taps her ear. "What was that?"

I lean in closer as she dances around me. "I'm Dylan, and you are?"

"Dancing." She breathes on a small laugh. "It's nice to meet you, Dylan."

"You've been watching me." I stand in place while the patrons of this club down around me, brushing against my expensive, imported suit.

She spins before she slows. "I could say the same for you."

I look down at her face.

Jesus, she's striking. Her eyes are a shade of blue, that particular shade of blue that always takes my breath away.

"We're leaving together tonight."

That cocks one of perfectly arched brows. "You're assuming that not I'm leaving with someone else."

"You're here alone." I spin when she does to catch her gaze again.

The skirt of her black dress picks up with the motion revealing a beautiful set of legs. "Maybe I like being alone."

"Not tonight." I reach for her hand.

She slows before she slides her palm against mine. "Dance with me, Dylan."

I breathe out on a heavy sigh. I haven't heard those four words in years. I haven't danced in as long.

I pull her close to me, sliding my free hand down her back. "What's your name?"

"Does it matter?" She looks up at me.

It never does.

I dance her closer to an alcove, a spot where the crowd is thin and the music quieter.

Her body follows mine instinctively, our shared movements drawing the admiring glances of others.

She's letting me lead now, but the sureness of her steps promises aggression in bed.

"We're wasting time. "

Her lips curve up into a smile. "Foreplay comes in many forms."

"Is that what this is?" I laugh. "I want to fuck you."

She presses every inch of her body against me. "You will."

My cock swells with those words. "Now."

"Patience, Dylan." Her lips brush my jawline. "I promise this will be a night you'll never forget."

Coming Soon

THANK YOU

Thank you for purchasing my book. I can't even begin to put to words what it means to me. If you enjoyed it, please remember to write a review for it. Let me know your thoughts! I want to keep my readers happy.

For more information on new series and standalones, please visit my website, **www.deborahbladon.com**. There are book trailers and other goodies to check out.

If you want to chat with me personally, please LIKE my page on Facebook. I love connecting with all of my readers because without you, none of this would be possible.

www.facebook.com/authordeborahbladon

Thank you, for everything.

ABOUT THE AUTHOR

Deborah Bladon has never read a romance hero she didn't like. Her love for romance novels began when she was old enough to board the bus, library card in hand to check out the newest Harlequin paperbacks. She's a Canadian by heart, and by passport, but you can often spot her in New York City sipping a latte and looking for inspiration for her next story. Manhattan is definitely her second home.

She cherishes her family and believes that each day is a gift for writing, for reading, and for loving.

CPSIA information can be obtained
at www.ICGtesting.com
Printed in the USA
FSHW021938250219
55946FS